22085

£2·50

JET SMOKE AND DRAGON FIRE

JET SMOKE
AND
DRAGON FIRE

CHARLES ASHTON

WALKER BOOKS
LONDON

For Ben

First published 1991 by Walker Books Ltd
87 Vauxhall Walk, London SE11 5HJ

© 1991 Charles Ashton

Printed in Great Britain by
Billings and Sons Ltd, Worcester

British Library Cataloguing in Publication Data
Ashton, Charles
Jet smoke and dragon fire.
I.Title
823'.914 [F]

ISBN 0-7445-2210-2

CONTENTS

THE SEARCH FOR
THE STONE

Sparrow could remember five occasions when Ms Minn had taken one of her "turns" and marched off into the mountains. The last time was when he had found Murie's milkstone. The next time it happened, his whole life changed.

Poor Ms Minn, poor old stick – that was what parents said; but as far as their children were concerned, her "turns" were something to look forward to, because they meant a holiday of weeks, or even months, before the old creature tottered back from wherever she had been and clanged the school bell once more.

"She's going," Sparrow whispered to Bull. "I can feel it. She's cracking."

Bull tapped his head. "This'll be a one-monther, at least," he whispered back.

On Sparrow's other side there was a crash as Gogs' tower of coins teetered and fell all over the floor. Gogs' curly red head went down as he scrambled for them. His nose came up over the edge of Sparrow's seat. "This'll be a one-monther," he whispered, grinning his biggest Gogs-grin.

Last time – the time when Sparrow found the milkstone – Ms Minn's departure had been quite dramatic. She had tipped over the desks and stamped on the calculators before storming off in floods of tears. The calculators had seemed undamaged – not that anyone would have known either way – but the carpenter had had to be called in to repair some of the desks. That had been a four-month holiday, the longest Sparrow could remember.

Today Ms Minn had them haul out the boxes of copper coins. First of all they had to sort out the ones with women's heads on them from the ones with men's heads. The girls took the women's-head coins and the boys took the men's-head ones, and then they had to make towers on their desks. Ms Minn went round the class admiring their teetering spires of money. Occasionally she poked one and sent it crashing to ruin on the floor.

Just before lunch, she suddenly asked, "Does anyone know how to tell the time?" There were a lot of strange looks as everyone tried to work out what she meant. "Very well," she went on, "I'll tell you. Everyone cover their eyes. Now –

'At the third stone
The time has come...'"

Everyone waited. "That's it," said Ms Minn brightly. "Time for lunch."

But late in the afternoon she stopped and moaned and stood wringing her hands, like a bony old scarecrow in her dusty black dress. The paper-thin skin of her face puckered in an expression of unspeakable sorrow. "Oh," she groaned, "oh – oh – oh no, that's enough, that's quite enough..."

Everyone became very quiet. A far-away look came into the old teacher's mild face, while her pale brown eyes seemed to film over like tar in a puddle. "All right," she said decisively, "I'm coming." And she turned and left the classroom.

An excited buzz of talk broke out, and there was a scraping and a scrambling as chairs were pushed back and coats were fetched and holidays were thought about.

Soon afterwards, people saw Ms Minn clumping off in her big boots, a black scraggle under the autumn-golden trees by the road out of the village. Her wild white hair flamed in the sunset and her coat flapped like a washing-line of rags. No one who saw her thought much about it: Ms Minn had been the teacher at the village school for as long as anyone could remember, and for as long as anyone could remember she had been having her "turns". No one knew where she went, but as she always seemed to come back safely enough, no one was much worried about her.

Sparrow, Bull and Gogs followed her shortly afterwards. Their homes were outside the village, on three little rounded green hills that rose beside the Old Road: Gogs' first, then Bull's, and Sparrow's the last of the three. All the way up the steep, cobbled street that led out of the village, the three friends shuffled fallen leaves and argued about how long their holiday would be, and what they would do during it; but by the time they got to the foot of Gogs' path they had got no further than agreeing to meet on the railway track the next day.

In the light of the sunset of that last ordinary day of his life, Sparrow panted up the white-pebbled path to the top of his own hill, and came in sight of the thatched roof of his house. The great rounded mountain peak that loomed over the valley glowed gold-rose as the sun sank. Over the roof, the forest climbed towards the mountain's stony base in tangled folds and hummocks from the small, hilly fields where he and Murie had gathered the last of their harvest two weeks before. He trotted on down between the tall kale plants in the vegetable garden, stopped to tickle the tummy of a large ginger cat stretched on the seat outside the front door and passed into the wood-panelled hallway where his father's crossbow and quiver of bolts still hung, polished and greased, on the wall.

"Is that you, Sparrow?" Murie, his mother, called through to the living room, where Sparrow had paused in front of the television. "You'll need to get wood from the coalshed."

"School's stopped," Sparrow called back absently, gazing at the blank grey screen. "Ms Minn's off again."

"Poor old thing," Murie's voice came back. "I don't know how she keeps going."

Sparrow's eyes fell on the milkstone, glowing coolly from the shadows in its place on the top of the television, and a thought struck him.

The railway line was a favourite place for the boys. Over a good deal of its length lower down in the valley, the village people had lifted the rails from the sleepers and melted them down to make knives or ploughs or grates for their fires; but higher up, where the line climbed off into the mountains, it had been left untouched. The metal was rusted, and amongst the stones on the bed of the track skinny weeds poked up, and a strange, acrid smell always hung faintly in the air. It was a desolate, mysterious thing, stretching off through the rocky, green-grown land, and no adults ever came there.

Sparrow minced along the flat, rusty top of one of the rails, one foot in front of the other, holding out his arms to either side to balance himself. "Anyway, I do know what an aeroplane looks like," he said, continuing an argument they had been having before.

"Go on then, tell us," challenged Bull, whose grandmother had told them there was no such thing.

"It's like a sort of tube with wings like birds' – only they don't flap – out to the sides like this," said Sparrow, flapping his hands up and down on the ends of his outstretched arms. "And people sit inside the tube."

"You said that their wings didn't flap," remarked Gogs.

"I was just showing you," Sparrow dropped his arms and immediately lost his balance and slipped off the rail. "Anyway, I know, because my grandad used to say he flew in one once, when he was very young."

Bull snorted. "If there was such a thing, my gran would know all about it. She says there're no stories about them at all."

"I didn't say they were a story. My grandad really flew in one."

"So why didn't my gran?" said Bull.

"Or mine," added Gogs.

In most things Sparrow would not have dared to suggest that anyone could ever have known more than Bull's grandmother. For one thing, Bull's gran had brought Bull up because both his mother and father were dead, and neither Sparrow nor Gogs liked to offend Bull by saying anything against her. But for another thing, old Mrs Hind really did know a lot that no one else in the village knew. She had told Bull some of her old stories, but she always said, "Now keep that to yourself, so it doesn't get out," and Bull would do as she said – except that, very occasionally, he would tell Sparrow and Gogs a little of what he had learned.

"There's dragons," said Gogs pleasantly, trying to head off an argument.

"What about dragons?" Bull snapped.

"There's dragons in stories," Gogs said.

"So?" said Bull, with scorn. "Dragons are animals. They may be magic, but they're still animals: they're real things, not stupid flying tubes."

Bull, with his black hair and his piercing blue eyes that stared unblinking from under fierce, knotted eyebrows, never let his friends forget that he knew more than they did, or ever would. It was through him that they had learned that there was such a thing as magic, and he always talked as if he knew many dark secrets. This made him the accepted leader of the three friends.

Sparrow shrugged. "Anyway, I'm only saying what my grandad said," he mumbled.

"Are we going to hunt rabbits?" Gogs said. "That's what my dad said we should do."

Then Sparrow remembered his idea from the night before and forgot about his grandad's aeroplane.

"It's Murie's birthday tomorrow," he said, "and I wanted to try and find another milk-stone to go with the first one."

Bull's scowling face brightened. "I'll help you look," he said promptly.

"Me too," said Gogs, "though Sparrow's the best stone-finder there is."

That was true, and even Bull had to admit it. Milkstones, with their delicate gold veins and their white, smooth surface, were very rare, and Sparrow had found the only one in recent times. The only place they could be found was the Cliff of Stones, and the three friends immediately set off through the bright thickets of golden birch and red rowan that climbed towards the deep shade of the pine forest on the lower slopes of the mountains.

In the mid-morning they reached the Cliff. You came on it very suddenly, rearing sixty metres above the dense-packed pine forest, grey-brown, full-face towards the sun. Against the lower half of it there was a heap of loose stones and dust which became steadily steeper, till at one end of the Cliff the land plunged away in screes and rock-falls down towards the Forest River.

The three friends started working along beneath the towering precipice. The morning mists had cleared away and the autumn heat shimmered over the rock.

"There's always amethysts," said Bull after

a little. Sweat was pouring off his face.

Gogs' fair skin was beetroot-red. "I bet that's full of amethyst," he said, holding out a lump of rock the size of a small turnip.

Sparrow took the lump and tapped it doubtfully. "I don't think so," he said.

Gogs spent the next ten minutes trying to break open the rock by banging it on other rocks, only to find that Sparrow had, as usual, been right. Disheartened, he sat down, pulled round a leather bag attached to his belt, and fished a squashy parcel out of it. "I'm going to have some lunch," he announced.

Bull sat down beside him. He had food with him too. "I never thought of bringing anything to eat," Sparrow said, "and I'm really quite hungry."

"You'd forget your own ears if they weren't tied on with string," said Bull.

"You'd forget your own legs if your mam didn't stick your body on to them in the morning," said Gogs.

Sparrow accepted their rebuke silently, and Bull spared him a sandwich while Gogs gave him an apple. But not long after they had eaten, Bull and Gogs said they had had enough of stone-searching. They tried to persuade Sparrow to go back with them, but Sparrow went vague, as he always did when his mind was set on something.

"I'll just check along this bit," he murmured,

stooping, picking up the stones, turning them over, searching left and right. After a little, Gogs and Bull realized he wasn't coming at all, and started off through the trees.

"We'll tell your mam you forgot your balance and fell off the cliff!" they called cheerfully.

Sparrow only half heard. "I'll just check ten more stones," he told himself, "then I'll follow them, and Murie will have to have one of the amethysts."

But ten stones were picked up and then thrown down again, and another ten, and another, and soon Sparrow had forgotten all about Gogs and Bull, and searched on alone through the silent afternoon.

The boys were not supposed to go to the steep edge of the scree at the end of the Cliff, and as Sparrow worked his way along the cliff-foot, the sound of the river far below reached his ears, deep and drumming, and he knew he was very near the forbidden place. He flattened himself on the ground, crawling forwards on his stomach to peer over.

As he peeped out over the broken rocks, he knocked a stone over the edge. He watched as it bounced and bounded down the drop until it disappeared into the forest gloom.

Looking down the slope where the stone had gone, Sparrow noticed something amongst the grey trunks. He squinted harder, but after

16

frowning and squinting for quite some time, all
he knew for certain was that there was a *shape*
down there – bundled on the ground, difficult
to make out because it was almost the same
colour as the forest floor under the shadow of
the trees.

He peered and peered, creeping out further
than he should have – even for someone lying
on his stomach – to the very edge of the drop.
In a little while he became certain that the
shape he was looking at was the shape of a
man huddled up on the earth, lying quite still.

That was when the whole thing suddenly
became very strange. Sparrow was looking
down on the man's shape from high above. He
was almost too far away even to be sure it was
a man and not a tree trunk or a large boulder.
And all the time the noise of the waterfall
down below filled the air, too loud for any
other sound to be heard. Yet as Sparrow
watched, the shape below became clearer and
clearer. He gazed, lost in total concentration,
and gradually made out that it was a man
dressed in a long green-brown coat with a
hood covering his head.

As soon as he realized this – almost as if it
had been waiting for him – the head moved,
and the face under the hood became visible.
Sparrow caught his breath, and the hairs on
the back of his neck prickled. It was a face wild
and old and wrinkled, with tangled grey hair

17

all about it; but glinting through the hair were piercing green eyes – eyes green as birch-leaves, as wild as a windy day. For just a moment, Sparrow thought he had seen that face before, but then the mouth moved, and a quiet voice said – as clearly as if it had spoken right beside his ear – "Boy, come down here to me: I need your help."

THE GIFT

Sparrow had to go a long way round to get down to the place where the old man lay: through the woods in front of the Cliff of Stones until he found the Forest River; then along beside the river until it fell away spuming and foaming over the jagged rocks of the waterfall; then up again through the trees at the foot of the steep scree.

But the old man wasn't difficult to find. Sparrow almost walked straight into him.

As soon as he saw him, Sparrow realized that he was not able to walk: one of his legs was so badly twisted that it was almost behind his back. "I fell," he grumbled. "Silly old goat."

Sparrow said nothing. He knew the old man wanted his help – he had asked for it, anyway – but he wasn't sure what he could do. He certainly could not carry him!

"Well then, well then, don't just stand there," the old man chided, "that won't do any good."

"Shall I pull you up?" Sparrow said.

The old man spluttered under his hood, and his eyes glinted like sunlight rippling through the trees. "Pull me up? He wants to pull me up!" he gasped to himself. Then, looking Sparrow full in the face – Sparrow again felt a shiver running up his spine at the glint of those wild forest eyes – "Twenty strong men couldn't lift me up, young one," he chuckled, "not even if they were yoked to a strong team of oxen."

"I think just one strong man could pull you up," said Sparrow, who was beginning to wonder if the old man might be a little crazy. "In fact, I think I could pull you up, if it wouldn't hurt you."

"One strong man, eh?" the old man said. "Or one skinny little fellow no taller than a salt-barrel. Come on then, give it a go and you'll see." He held out his hand with a chuckle.

Sparrow took it. It felt strange – cold, and not quite like a hand: more like a piece of polished wood, maybe.

Sparrow dug his feet into a tussock and pulled. Nothing moved. The old man's grip on his own hand didn't seem particularly tight, but Sparrow had the strange feeling of being pulled downwards. He grasped the old man's wrist with his other hand and heaved for all he was worth, digging his feet firmer into the damp grassy ground. There wasn't the slightest hint of a movement: it was as though he were hauling at the branch of an ancient tree with roots that reached deep into the earth. It wasn't that the old man was too heavy to move: more that he was a part of something that simply *didn't* move. Sweat broke out on Sparrow's forehead; his whole body was taut like a bent bow; he felt as if his arms were being tugged out of their sockets. A high-pitched grunt broke from between his clenched teeth, and just then the ground gave way. The grassy tussock broke under his feet, his shoes skidded forwards over mud and he sat down *bump*, on his bottom, with a shock that jarred his whole back.

The old man hooted with laughter. He coughed and wheezed and spluttered till Sparrow forgot all about his sore bottom and began to worry that the other would choke with laughing.

"Not bad! Not bad!" the old man gasped at last. "You almost shifted my left little toe. You're stronger than you think. You might even move a mountain some day. But you can't move me. No one can move me!"

Sparrow got up slowly, rubbing his bottom. He was quite convinced that the old man was mad now, yet it was true enough, he hadn't been able to move him.

"How can I help you then?" he asked.

"That's more like it," the old man murmured. "Questions are better than answers." He looked Sparrow slowly up and down. Then he remarked, "You are in a dream."

"Yes, I think I must be," Sparrow agreed, scratching his head.

"Not in the way you think," the old man said. "You couldn't move me because you are a dream-thing and I am not."

Sparrow did not much like the sound of this, but he said nothing.

"Well, listen," the old man said, "I said I was a silly old goat and that's just exactly what I am. I came out without my stick, I did, and now I've gone and fallen down through the trees and broken my leg."

Sparrow didn't understand what the old man meant by saying that he had "fallen down through the trees", so all he said was, "Where is your stick?"

"Well, listen," the old one said again. "What you have to do is follow the little dark stream up to its source. You'll come to it if you go down beside the river for a little bit. When you get to its source, there's a cave, and in the cave there's my stick."

As the old man described it, Sparrow had a clear picture in his mind of the cave, and a strange bent stick of dark, polished wood leaning against its back wall.

The old man nodded, almost as if he could

see the picture that Sparrow was seeing. "That's right," he chuckled. "Now, there's just one thing about my stick: it'll try to play tricks on you. But don't you let it. You remember it's just a stick you're fetching me, and you'll manage well enough."

A short way below the place where he had found the old man, Sparrow came upon the little dark stream running down the hillside in a deep channel among the straight, slender grey trunks of a young ash wood. Keeping as close to it as he could, he started the ascent. By the time he had climbed through the ash wood to where the rocky mountain heights towered above him, he saw from the sun that it had become late. He realized sadly that he would probably not manage to get a stone for Murie at all now.

Up and up Sparrow climbed, and always the little dark stream murmured softly beside him. Soon he was higher in the mountains than he had ever been before, climbing over short grass in a flat space between two rocky walls, with the little dark stream flowing quietly through the greenest part of the grass.

Here and there ivy grew, covering the rock walls, and it was eventually into a solid mass of ivy that the little dark stream disappeared. Sparrow forced his way through the thick, cool leaves, and found that the ivy was growing over a cleft in the rock wall just wide

23

enough for him to squeeze through.

He emerged into a circular space: a mountain courtyard with frowning rock walls on every side. Through the courtyard the little dark stream rustled, and in the very centre was the place where it bubbled up through the ground from under some flat, silvery stones. Straight across from it, Sparrow saw the triangle-shape of a cave mouth in the rock wall.

The cave had furniture in it, and was very like an ordinary room. There was a low fire in the grate, a chair beside the fire, a bed in one corner, a table in the middle and shelves with something on them that Sparrow didn't recognize, for the simple reason that he had never seen a book before.

He saw the stick straight away, and was glad that he wouldn't have to look for it, for he found the cave just a little bit spooky. He crossed over to where the stick was leaning against the wall, and was about to take it when – *sssss!* He found he had made a horrible mistake: it was not a stick at all, but a snake! Brown with vivid red markings in a zig-zag down its back, it was the thickness of Sparrow's leg, and its wedge-like expressionless face and blank golden eyes were turned full on him. It must have been hanging down from something on the wall, Sparrow thought as, frozen to the spot with fear, he watched the thing slither down into great heavy coils on the floor. Its head swayed slowly, stretching out towards him, the tongue flickering from the slit of its mouth.

Sparrow's hair stood all on end, and he turned and bolted. He didn't stop till he was right outside the cave, in the middle of the courtyard of rocks, with the little dark stream bubbling out from the stones at his feet. There he waited, expecting to see the snake slithering out of the cave at any moment.

But the snake did not come. Above his head, the colour was draining out of the sky: sunset could be no more than half an hour off. Sparrow's thoughts turned again to the old man's instructions. He forced himself, reluctantly, back to the triangle-shaped cave mouth, and peered in fearfully, watching for the snake but at the same time looking round to see if he could make out the stick leaning against some other wall.

How strange: there, against the wall right in front of him, was the stick he had first seen. Twisted and bent, and all of smooth dark polished wood – the same stick he had pictured when the old man had told him about it!

Then he remembered what the old man had said about the stick playing tricks on him. Of course, he thought, there never was any snake at all! His fear left him in a rush. He could almost have laughed.

In he went, and over to the stick. He put his hands on his hips and said to it, "Stick, you think you can play tricks on me! Well, you can't, because I know all about you." And then he took hold of it.

For a moment he felt it in his hand – just for a moment, and then suddenly: *splash!* He was holding nothing at all, but a big splat of water had hit the stone floor, making him leap back with wet legs. Out of nowhere the water had come, and now it was beginning to trickle off into the cracks between the stones.

This time, however, Sparrow was more ready for it. "Oh no, you don't!" he cried, falling to his knees and starting to gather all the water together in a puddle before it disappeared. "You may look like water, but I know you're a stick, and I can see you, I can see you, I can see you!" As he spoke he thought as hard as he could about the stick leaning up against the wall.

And suddenly, there it was again, leaning calmly against the wall as if it had never moved – and the floor was quite dry!

Now Sparrow was more careful. He just held out his hand a little way from the stick, and spoke to it, as if he were coaxing a cat out of a hidey-hole. "Are you coming?" he said. "The old man needs you and he told me to fetch you." Sparrow vaguely wondered if he was starting to crack as well, because he had

certainly never heard of being polite to a stick
before. But it seemed to work. The stick stood
up from the wall, all by itself, and toppled
gently into his outstretched hand.

The smooth wood felt pleasant to hold, and
Sparrow stroked it gently as he walked back
out of the cave. But just as he was crossing the
courtyard towards its ivy-grown entrance, the
stick spoke to him.

Sparrow knew it was the stick speaking,
because it jerked in his hand. "Who do you
think you are," it said, "carrying me about as
if you owned me – and stroking my head?"

"I'm Sparrow," said Sparrow. "I don't *think*
I'm Sparrow: that's who I *am*."

"Oh," retorted the stick scornfully, "he
knows who he is! Well –" And suddenly it
jerked right out of Sparrow's hand and span
round once, twice, three times and up into the
air, where it hung still about three metres
above his head.

"Well," it snapped, "what do you say now,
bonehead? Turnip-face?"

"I say, please can you come down and stay
in my hand," Sparrow said. "It's time for me
to go home now and I have to take you —"

But before he could finish what he was
saying – *whizz-whizz!* The stick started whirling
round and round, as though being twirled by an
invisible hand. Twenty times, maybe, it whirled,
then did a series of cartwheels that took it over

to the far side of the courtyard. And then it span around, and suddenly came flying straight towards Sparrow – fast, purposeful, menacing as a spear aimed at his head. At the very last moment Sparrow ducked, and the stick crashed end-on into the rock wall and clattered on to the ground.

Sparrow really was a bit scared of it now. That was no joke, the way it had flown at him. Where would he be if he hadn't ducked?

But when he carefully picked it up, it just felt like any ordinary stick, and he decided it must have knocked itself senseless when it hit the rock, because it didn't say another word or try any more tricks on him. He reached the foot of the little dark stream, and a short while later was handing the stick carefully to the old man, who kept his wild green eyes fixed on Sparrow as he took it, stroking the polished wood and speaking quietly to it.

A moment later, the woods, the waterfall and the towering cliffs had all disappeared, and the old man, no longer crippled, was standing in front of Sparrow in the rocky mountain courtyard outside the cave.

Sparrow blinked. "Was that magic?" he asked.

"Magic's in the mind of the beholder," the old man said mysteriously. "Do you think it was magic?"

"Yes, I think I do," said Sparrow.

"Then magic it was," he answered. "And now, because you helped me, I'm going to give you three wishes."

"Me?" Sparrow echoed stupidly.

"Who else would he be speaking to, bone-head?" snapped the stick. "Himself?" But the old man slapped it sharply on the head and told it to be quiet. In fact, the old man seemed to be a lot calmer and more sensible now he was holding the stick. But this time, although it was only the second time he had heard it speak, the stick's voice seemed to Sparrow oddly familiar: as though it belonged to someone he had known all his life...

"What's your name?" the old man asked.

Sparrow told him.

"You can call me Puckel," he said in return. "And now be quick and tell me what your three wishes are, for it's time you were home."

Sparrow felt embarrassed, not knowing what to ask for. Like most of the young folk of the mountains, he was quite content and didn't wish for anything he didn't have. It required immense thought, wishing for something. Yet, after all the strange things which had happened that afternoon, he felt quite sure that the old man with the wild grey hair and green eyes was perfectly able to give him whatever he asked.

"Well," Sparrow said slowly, "I was trying to find a special white stone with gold in it for Murie..."

"Oh, oh, oh!" exclaimed Puckel excitedly. "But you don't need magic for that! Look for the stone, and you'll find it – don't come asking me! Think! Think! Think! Think back over one day! There's a hundred wishes you have in each hour!"

Sparrow found that hard to believe, but he did think back over everything that had happened that day. Most of the day had been taken up with looking for the stone, and the old man didn't seem to think that was worth wishing for. He thought of Bull and Gogs. Seeing an aeroplane? Was that worth wishing for? Sitting inside an aeroplane? He tried to imagine that... Looking into the bright, brilliant blue of the sky; somewhere far below, little mountains etched with snowy peaks... Almost as if someone else were using it, Sparrow heard his voice saying, "I would like to fly." Immediately afterwards he seemed to get control of it again, and added doubtfully, "But I don't really know if I could do that."

"You don't know? But of course you could!" Puckel laughed.

He planted his stick firmly on the ground and vaulted over to stand in front of Sparrow. Then he held out his arms, and his broad green-brown coat covered Sparrow's face. It smelled of the woods, of new leaves, of dying grasses, of toadstools in a damp hollow.

"Let him fly," he murmured. "Let him fly,

30

let him fly. Be eagle, be swallow, be wild goose – be Sparrow." Stepping back he said, "And what else? That's only one wish."

"I don't really know what else," said Sparrow, now feeling very stupid. "That's all I can think of."

"Well, well and well again," old Puckel said. "There's a lad who'll never go far. Can't think what he wants, eh? Then you'll have to watch out for unkind spirits. Well, I'll tell you what. One wish you've had. Now go home and think, and when you've thought, come back and call for me, why not? Then I'll give you what you ask for."

"Thank you," said Sparrow.

"Oh, don't thank me," Puckel said, as if to himself. "You brought me my stick, and now I'm under an obligation to you, a great obligation. Not many could have brought me that stick, yet you passed the test without hesitation. But now –" and he was no longer speaking to himself "– think hard, and think right, and don't let yourself be fooled by unkind spirits that aren't what they seem. Come back soon – and now, fly!"

Sparrow didn't know what the old man meant about the unkind spirits. But he soon knew that he could fly, for with one great spring he leapt up into the air – and simply hung there, weightless, six dizzy metres above the ground.

He found himself peering over the top of the rock wall round the mountain courtyard, and the angle of the steep mountainside seemed all wrong. He moved his head, and rock wall and mountainside tilted alarmingly to one side, uphill and downhill suddenly changing places. He put out a hand to steady himself and found he was clutching at thin air. He panicked, the whole world rolled right round, and a second later he was looking straight down into the courtyard of Puckel's cave. He had rolled over on to his front, and he was floating: the ground didn't come any closer.

The old man had apparently gone back into his cave without another glance. Sparrow took a deep breath. "It's real," he muttered. "It's all right." He stretched out his arms in front of him, straightened his legs, and something like a shock seemed to take his whole body. He felt like one single piece of bone – a hollow bird's bone with no weight – and he soared upwards, forwards, without effort, while a fierce wind rumbled in his ears and tore at his hair without lessening his speed. He was flying, and didn't know how he was doing it. Higher, and higher again, and he was looking over an impossible stretch of mountain and forest, where everything seemed somehow to have been flattened out.

In the distance, hollowed under the luminous air, he could see the clutter of shapes and shades that was the village and the three round green hills (little tufts, they were more like from here) where his and his friends' houses stood; and the sun was just setting over the mountains on the far side of the valley.

"Whee! Whee! Whoopee!" he called, for the impossible, giddy joy of being fifty metres up in the air without a thought of falling. Then he sped down towards the distant valley, and the ground rushed up terrifyingly towards him. He bowed his back inwards, and his flight immediately levelled out. Below him the rocks of the high ground rushed past, then the pine forests like a dull green mist, till a lurch of the ground beneath him told him he had passed the Cliff where he had searched for a stone.

Sparrow threw his head back and came upright, suddenly breaking his headlong flight. The air whooshed up round him and grew still again. He hung there like a hawk, looking back at the Cliff, for he had caught a glimpse of something that shone and sparkled.

There it was. The last light of the setting sun was picking out a stone, high up on the Cliff, too high and too steep to be reached by climbing. It shone creamy-white, rose-white with the sunset. Sparrow flew straight to it, and hovering close, he reached out and pulled it from the loose rock.

It was a milkstone – just the very kind he had spent all day looking for. As big as his hand, milky white, and streaked with delicate flakes of gold. It was more than a companion for Murie's stone that sat on the television: it was the most beautiful milkstone Sparrow had ever seen.

THREE WEEKS ALONE

It was strange approaching his home from the air. As Sparrow came down to land on top of the green hill, he was aware that old Puckel's gift would change everything. He seemed to be looking with new eyes at the long, thatched house with its faded white walls and small windows where he had lived all his life. It was as if he were noticing it for the first time. And the fields, forests and mountains rising behind looked new and strange, mysterious and full of things he had never even dreamed existed.

Sparrow landed rather clumsily, tripping over his feet and nearly falling. For a second he thought he couldn't move, until he realized that he was simply feeling the weight of his body which had been left behind when he was flying. Then the cold hit him: it occurred to him for the first time that he had felt none of the autumn-evening chill when he was air-borne. He shivered, and at the same time his face burned from the wind that had been blowing into it. There was a drumming in his ears still, but after listening to it for a moment Sparrow realized it wasn't the wind: there was a snorting and whickering mixed with it, and he saw Cairo, his father's ancient horse, careering round the paddock behind the house as if a swarm of bees were after him. Cairo was a stiff-jointed, ill-natured old beast who had never let anyone near him since Sparrow's father had disappeared, and he never moved faster than a sulky hobble. Now he was bucking and swerving around the field like a colt, and Sparrow understood that it must have been the sight of him flying which set the horse off. He laughed, and went indoors.

Before going through to the kitchen, Sparrow softly moved the old milkstone from the middle of the television top to the left-hand side. On the right-hand side he placed the new stone.

"I always seem to find them when Ms Minn goes away," he murmured – not quite accurately, since it was only the second milkstone he had found. "Perhaps it's the bits of her brain that keep falling out..." Murie would never notice the new stone in the darkness that evening, and it would be there to surprise her when she came downstairs on her birthday morning.

Murie had given up trying to prepare the evening meal in the long-waned daylight from the window, and was just placing the glass bowl over the second of the two yellow-gleaming wall-lamps as Sparrow came in. The soft beam from the lamps fell across the homely things in the kitchen which had always been the centre of Sparrow's world: yellow on the solid, well-scrubbed pine table by the window; coppery on the great brown-grey clay stove with its black-iron cooking range built into the front; yellow-gleaming on the huge black pot in which Murie was cooking tomorrow's potatoes for the goat, cow and hens; distant, jewel-like yellow in the depths of the milky-white glass onion that hung on a cord from the ceiling and was always referred to as "the light", even though it never gave out more than a vague reflection...

There was a mingled smell of boiling potatoes, pea-and-duck soup, and honey cake. "I'm starving," Sparrow said, making Murie jump.

"Where have you been all day?" she said. "You've not had any lunch."

"I got some from Bull and Gogs," Sparrow said, "but not enough."

"You should have said; I'd have given you sandwiches. You're such a scatter-brain." Crossly she sloshed soup into bowls standing ready at the stove.

"Bull wouldn't believe that Grandad flew in an aeroplane," Sparrow said.

"Nor do I," Murie answered, plonking the bowls of soup, along with two hunks of fresh bread, on the table. "It's just a daft story he used to invent. Eat up."

Sparrow lived alone with his mother. His father had been lost around the same time as Bull's father, when the boys were still babies; but everyone knew what had happened to Bull's father, who had been killed by a horse high up on the Old Road, while Sparrow's father had simply disappeared. He had not been a Trader, like Bull's father, but had hunted, though higher into the mountains than most men of the village, who rarely went more than five or six kilometres from home. But he had not been hunting – at least, not with his crossbow – on the day he disappeared. What had happened to him no one knew, but in that land of fearsome cliffs and crashing waterfalls people did sometimes disappear, and it was supposed that he had slipped on the edge of some precipice and fallen to his death.

"Where were you?" Murie asked as they ate.

"Up at the railway line," Sparrow answered vaguely.

"Not too far, I hope," she said sharply. Sparrow shook his head, but kept his face down.

If Sparrow had stopped to think about it, he

would have noticed one immediate change which came from his amazing gift: overnight he became secretive. He told no one, neither Murie, nor Bull, nor Gogs. Without altogether realizing it, he was revelling in having a secret from Bull. For three long weeks after Murie's birthday, while autumn changed gradually to winter, he was on his own and flew so much his feet hardly ever touched the ground.

Every morning he would run off to a quiet clearing in the woods. There he would leap into the air and with a single bound find himself hovering beside the tops of the trees, with the seas of sodden, russet-leaved forests stretching away over his shoulders. Further up, through the rain, and a sudden new country would open beneath him, a country furrowed and ridged, pearl-coloured: the cloud-country, pierced by countless humped islands that were the mountain-tops.

High he could go, into the huge silences of the sky – or else he would skim low over the forest and send showers of frightened birds scattering, or he would race to the top of the tallest mountain, stand on the edge of the highest cliff and throw himself into the yawning gulf of air beneath him.

By flying, by going up into the high places, Sparrow learned a lot about the country he lived in – things he would never have learned at the village school even if he had gone there for fifty years. He learned about the mountains, which seemed to stretch endlessly on over towards the east, but which towards the west soon came to an end at a flat calm lake bordered by low hills; about the other villages, which he vaguely knew of but which no one talked of or went to (apart from the Traders, but no one talked of them either). Sparrow found out all there was to know about these villages, though to be sure that was not much. There were four of them, apart from his own, but all as near the same as his own as any four places could be. The railway line went through two of them, then it curved and snaked off towards the flat lake. Sparrow followed it on one occasion, but there were no farms or villages in that part of the country. There were no living trees either, though there were plenty of dead ones, and the ground was a nasty grey colour with very little grass. Something about the lake-side felt unpleasant: Sparrow told himself he wasn't scared of it, but he didn't go there again.

In the other direction, the railway line disappeared into a tunnel in the mountains, and Sparrow could find no further trace of it: there was no other end to the tunnel. Nor did he ever find what lay beyond the mountains: always, on the edge of the horizon, there was a curious bank of white mist where the mountain peaks faded from sight. It seemed to move slightly, as cloud does, but it never cleared, not even on the windiest of days. Sparrow tried several times to reach it, but it never seemed to come any closer.

Not surprisingly, Bull and Gogs werc meanwhile feeling rather neglected by Sparrow. Gogs did wonder at first if Sparrow might have been offended that day under the Cliff when they had gone off and left him. But it was not like Sparrow to stay offended for quite so long – he had never had a good enough memory for it. Gogs and Bull came over for him several times, but he was never in.

"Where do you go all by yourself?" Murie asked. "And what do you do?"

"Oh, I just go up to the woods and look at things," Sparrow answered vaguely.

"What sort of things?"

"Rocks and things." It was true enough – he just didn't mention that he was looking at rocks and things from way up in the air!

"How on earth did you manage to get that home?" Murie exclaimed, looking in amazement at the huge branch of a tree Sparrow had brought home one evening to cut up for the fire.

"I don't know," Sparrow said. "I just dragged it." In a way, that was true too: he didn't know how he had managed it – it was true that he had found that things didn't seem

41

to weigh anything when he was flying. It was as though his own lightness got into whatever he touched.

One morning Murie, out in their top field, noticed which way Sparrow was heading amongst the trees. Later that morning, Bull and Gogs came up the hill. They had decided to try to visit Sparrow once more and ask him if he had stopped being their friend altogether. On this occasion, Murie was able to tell them where she thought he had gone.

"You'll be getting quite fed up with him," she said. "I don't know what's got into him: I hardly ever see him either."

"We'll sort him out," Gogs grinned, as they set off along the side of Cairo's paddock. The old horse watched them sourly from the far end.

The two friends came to the clearing. Sparrow wasn't there, so they sat down on a log and wondered what to do next. Although the sun was bright, it was low over the tops of the mountains and the air already had a wintry chill.

"I'm not going to sit here all day," Bull said crossly.

"Nor me," said Gogs. "I'm freezing."

They were lucky, however. Sparrow had forgotten to collect the hens' eggs before he left, and had then remembered half-way through the morning and was flying back just as Bull and Gogs were deciding not to sit around.

Without noticing anyone in the clearing, he came down from the air, landed lightly on his feet, and stood still for a moment. He always did that now when he landed, to get used to the feelings of weight and cold that hit him.

But almost at once, something told him that he was not alone. He turned round to see the astonished faces of Gogs and Bull staring across at him.

For a full minute Gogs and Bull stared, pop-eyed as startled rabbits; and for a full minute there was silence in the clearing.

Sparrow looked at Bull, whose eyebrows were drawn so tightly together that they looked like a single bar of black across his forehead. He had a mixture of feelings. On the one hand, this was the moment he had been waiting for – the moment when he knew he had impressed Bull more than Bull had ever impressed him. On the other hand, he felt uneasy: he had never crossed Bull before. Without knowing what there was to be scared of, he felt a little scared.

Bull broke the silence. "You jumped down from the tree, didn't you?"

Sparrow shook his head. "No, I didn't," he said quietly.

There was another silence.

"You were flying?" Gogs said.

Sparrow nodded.

"No, he wasn't, Gogs," Bull said firmly.

"He's having us on. He jumped out of the trees."

"If he'd jumped out of the trees he'd have broken his legs," Gogs pointed out. It was not like Gogs to contradict Bull so sharply. "How did you learn to fly, Sparrow?" he asked.

"I was... Someone made me," Sparrow said. He didn't know how much he wanted to tell his friends. He had grown too used to being alone in the past weeks.

"Someone made you?" Bull repeated. "Do you mean you can't help doing it?"

"No," said Sparrow, "I only fly when I want to."

"How high do you go?" Gogs asked excitedly.

"However high I want to," Sparrow told him.

"Have you been far away?" Gogs asked. "Have you seen places we don't know about? Have you been to the end of the mountains?"

"Did someone teach you?" Bull interrupted.

"Not exactly," Sparrow said. The short moment of triumph was fading and the uneasiness was fading too, but he was beginning to realize that Bull was going to get the whole story out of him. He wouldn't have minded so much telling Gogs, because Gogs was just excited at the thought that someone could fly. But he felt cross at himself because he knew he couldn't stand up to Bull.

"Did you find a wizard or a magician or something like that," Bull said, "and he taught you how to fly? – Was that what happened?"

Bull had of course told Sparrow and Gogs only a few of his grandmother's tales. So Sparrow was completely flummoxed by what seemed like an amazing guess. How did Bull know? The two boys stared at each other, but Sparrow's eyes soon faltered and fell before Bull's keen gaze. Maybe Bull already knew all about such things.

"I don't know if he was a magician or a wizard," Sparrow muttered. "He just held his cloak out and said some words over me, and I could fly."

"Did you find him in trouble and help him?" Bull pursued. "Is that what happened?"

Again Sparrow was amazed at Bull's guess. "Have you met him too?" he asked.

"No, I haven't exactly met him," Bull said mysteriously. "What was his name?" he added.

Sparrow opened his mouth to tell him: he had just got as far as the "P" of "Puckel" – when he found he'd forgotten! It was very strange, considering he had thought of the old man and his name almost every day since he had started flying. Now his mind was a complete blank.

"It was – Puzzle or Piddle or something like that," he said vaguely. "I suddenly can't remember."

"How did you help him?" said Bull, still

45

fixing Sparrow with his blue, unswerving eyes.

"Yes, can we go and help him too?" Gogs burst in, seeing what Bull was getting at. "And then he'll teach us to fly as well and we can all fly together!"

Suddenly, after three weeks of being alone, Sparrow realized that he would love to do that. What did it matter about impressing Bull? He had enjoyed flying on his own, but what was the point of having something so secret that you couldn't share it with anyone?

But there seemed to be no way of making Gogs and Bull find the old man in trouble. It had just been a matter of luck when that had happened to Sparrow.

"He'd fallen through the trees," he told them, "and broken his leg. But it was only because he didn't have his stick with him. I don't think he'll leave his stick behind again – he'll be very careful now."

"Tell us everything that happened," Bull said.

As Sparrow talked, he found that he had been missing Gogs and Bull all the time, and had been longing to tell them the whole story. But whenever he came to say the old man's name he couldn't remember it – or only the beginning and the end – so they decided just to call him Piddle.

Sparrow came to the end of the story.

"And what were the other two wishes?" Bull asked.

Incredible as it may seem, Sparrow had actually forgotten about them! His memory was like that: if he had one important thing to think about, he concentrated so much on it that he simply stopped thinking about anything else.

"I didn't know what to wish for," he told Bull.

"So you threw them away? Two wishes?" Bull asked, his eyes wide with disbelief.

"Well, not really," Sparrow remembered. "He said I could go back and see him when I'd thought."

"You mean you still have two wishes to make?" Bull exclaimed.

"Hooray!" Gogs cried. "You can make a wish for me, and a wish for Bull, and then we'll all be able to fly!"

Sparrow had never thought of this. It seemed a wonderful idea.

"Let's go and find him right now," Gogs said, "and we'll all be flying by the evening!"

"No, I've a better idea," said Bull. "Sparrow can fly to him now, and we'll have our wishes by lunchtime."

"All right, I'll do it," said Sparrow, and he would have flown off there and then.

But Bull stopped him. "You haven't heard what we want yet," he said.

"I thought you wanted to fly," said Sparrow in surprise.

"Well, not just," Bull said. "I want you to

47

tell Piddle that I want to be a shape-shifter…"

"What's a shape-shifter?" asked Sparrow.

"Never mind," Bull said. "Just tell him I want to be a shape-shifter and I want to understand the language of beasts and birds."

"Oh, that's good," Gogs put in, "I'd like that too."

"Isn't that two wishes?" Sparrow asked.

"Not really," Bull answered, "and if you say it all very quickly – Bull wants to be a shape-shifter who can understand the language of beasts and birds – I'm sure Piddle will think it's just the one wish."

"All right," said Gogs. "Then will you say that Gogs wants to be a flyer who can understand the language of beasts and birds – very quickly, so that he thinks it's just one wish?"

"I'll try," said Sparrow, "but if I ask for those things, how will you be able to fly with us, Bull?"

Bull just smiled mysteriously. "Oh, I'll manage," he said. "Don't worry, you won't leave me behind."

So, in great excitement, Sparrow left them. He leaped into the air, and hung there a moment above their heads. Gogs gasped.

"Don't forget!" Bull called up.

"I won't!" Sparrow called back, and was off.

High in the air he went, straight towards the huge rounded peak of the great mountain that

stood over the valley. Puckel's cave was somewhere in the shoulders of that mountain.

Puckel's cave! The moment he sprang into
the air he had remembered the old man's name.
He realized there was something very odd
about this, but continued his flight nevertheless.

He looked down. There was the Cliff where
he had found Murie's stones, and the Forest
River and the waterfall below it. And there
was the little dark stream winding down
towards the river! Sparrow's eye followed it up
through the hillside into the crags and rock
walls of the mountain.

But though he peered and peered, he could
see no sign of the rocky courtyard outside
Puckel's cave, where the little dark stream
rose. He flew down, and hunted over the rocks
and through the ravines: but somehow, try as
he would, he could not make out the two ivy-
covered rocks he had squeezed between.

At last Sparrow flew right down to the foot
of the little dark stream at the Forest River. He
had an idea that if he followed the stream, just
as before, he might find what he was looking
for. He wouldn't fly, he wouldn't even skim: he
would go on his two feet, just as he had done
that first time.

It worked. Sparrow followed the little dark
stream up into the mountain, over the grassy
floor in between the climbing rock walls, and
at last found the place where it flowed out

between the two huge ivy-covered rocks. Minutes later he stood in the little rocky courtyard where the stream bubbled up from the stones. But all about there were only rocks. He turned round and round; there was no cave.

"What's wrong?" Sparrow said to himself. "I'm sure this is the right place."

Sparrow thought. What had he been told? "Come back soon," Puckel had said: maybe he'd come too late! Maybe he would never see Puckel again and Bull and Gogs would never be able to fly with him.

But what did "soon" mean, anyway? What else had he said?

"Go home and think" – that's what it was – "and when you've thought, come back and call me..."

Call me? Well, it was worth a try. Sparrow rounded his hands at his mouth and shouted, "Puckel!"

As the echoes of his shout faded, something happened. A large ivy-covered rock nearby in the rock wall made a splitting sound. *Crick*, it went, then *crack*, then *crick* again, and suddenly, just as though it had always been there, there was the ivy-grown entrance of the cave.

TWO THINGS AS IF
THEY WERE ONE

Out of the entrance something floated – something dark and thin. Puckel's stick wavered
gently towards Sparrow and remained sus-
pended in front of him like the bar of a gate.
Sparrow reached out and held it with both
hands.

With a sound like a short, stony laugh, the
stick took off, dragging Sparrow into the air.
He was more amused than frightened, thinking
the stick was just being mischievous. But when
it flew very close to the rock wall and suddenly
made a sharp mid-air turn, Sparrow's legs flew
out to the side and cracked painfully against
the rock. "Ow!" he cried, and decided to let go.

But he couldn't. His hands seemed to be
stuck to the wood.

"Good sticking power, that!" the stick cack-
led, and proceeded to drag him on a most
alarming ride, at high speed, close around the
wall of the courtyard. Again Sparrow banged
his legs on the rock, and yet again. And now

he realized that there was more malice than mischief in the thing's performance.

"Puckel!" he called again. But by this time he was so dizzy he couldn't see if the old man had come to answer his call. Suddenly the stick did another turn, and hovered in the air near the rock wall.

"What's the matter with you?" Sparrow gasped. "What have I done wrong?"

The stick made no answer, but jerked again into movement. Backwards this time and gathering speed at an amazing rate, it was hurling Sparrow towards the opposite wall of the courtyard. "Help!" Sparrow screamed. In a moment he would hit the rock wall, and then –

"Put him down." Puckel's voice was quiet, but it cut through the noise of the air whistling in Sparrow's ears. With a sharp jolt, the stick halted, so suddenly that Sparrow flew backwards to his arms' length. He felt his shoulder-sockets wrench, and then the stick let go of him – that was what it felt like anyway – and he fell to the ground. He felt dizzy and battered and sick.

He sat up and tried to look at Puckel. He had forgotten how wild the old man looked. At another word from him, the stick floated obediently down into his hand. He looked steadily at Sparrow. "Well," he said at last, quite ignoring the state Sparrow was in, "flying's been good, I see; it's been good, very good. I thought you would have been back to me a long time ago, asking for more – but flying was so good you forgot all about your other wishes."

"Yes, I did," agreed Sparrow, trying to focus his eyes.

"But now you've remembered about them?"

"Yes, I have," said Sparrow. "That's why I came back looking for you."

Puckel waited, looking hard at Sparrow. Sparrow began to feel better. He smiled weakly. It looked to him as though the old man were about to break into uncontrollable chuckling as at their first meeting, but he remained grave. He never actually smiled, Sparrow realized, but there was something about him as though all his insides were shaking with barely-suppressed mirth.

"Why were you so difficult to find?" Sparrow asked. He felt he'd been looking for Puckel for days.

"Because your brain's full of bone," the stick snapped, before Puckel could say anything.

Puckel slapped the stick on the head. But he was barely more polite himself. "Do you think I want every fool in the mountains coming and calling my name?" he said, turning towards the cave. "One's quite enough."

He passed out of sight through the cave mouth. Scared it might close again, Sparrow jumped up and followed him in. He felt better and his legs weren't sore any more, but he had no time to be surprised about that.

There was a brown stone bowl in the middle of the table in the cave, and Puckel was holding his stick over it as Sparrow came in. As he watched, the stick seemed to go soft, to melt and go smaller, and in a moment what Puckel was holding in his hands was water, which he allowed to pour gently into the bowl. Puckel looked intently at its black shining surface in the wavering light from the fire.

"I don't like what you're here for," he said suddenly.

"Can't I have my other two wishes?" Sparrow asked.

"Oh, you can have them," Puckel replied, "you can have them and welcome. I promised them, and I must give them. But they're bad wishes, and you'll be sorry you made them."

"But I haven't told you what they are yet!"

"You haven't told me, but now you will tell me," said Puckel, and waited.

"Well," said Sparrow, "Bull wants to be a shape-shifter and understand the language of beasts and birds, and Gogs wants to be able to understand the language of beasts and birds and fly. I thought they were asking for two things, but they said they weren't."

"Your wishes," said Puckel, looking up at Sparrow. "They are *your* wishes, not your friends'."

"I know," said Sparrow, "but..."

Puckel interrupted him. "They are good wishes. Shape-changing, and understanding the wild creatures and the tame creatures, the fish in the water, the bees gathering honey off the flowers. They are good wishes, yes."

"What's a shape-shifter anyway?" Sparrow asked.

Puckel disappeared. As Sparrow was looking about him, the chair by the fire suddenly spoke: "Come and sit on me." It was a strange voice, a little like Puckel's, but somehow stiffer, harder, more grating – a wooden voice, as though it were possible for Puckel to be speaking with a chair's voice.

Sparrow went and sat in the chair. It felt just like a chair and creaked as he sat down, but as he settled himself in it, the creaking became a muttering voice: "All right, all right, you needn't wiggle so much. What a great hefty wriggling lump you are! Goodness knows how you ever manage to fly..." A second later Puckel was standing in front of him again.

"Shape-changing," he said, "is the power of going into the shape of any other thing or creature, and becoming that creature for the length of the change. I was the chair. Now I am Puckel."

"Does that mean you can become an animal, too?" said Sparrow.

"As long as there's an animal to become. You

can't change into something that isn't there, unless you learn to step out of the dragon's dream and become a master of transformation. But a thing that's there – bird, beast, fish, fly, stone, chair, fire, water, cloud, ring, tree, book, bed, spider or speck of dust – any of these things you can become as a shape-changer, while your own shape disappears."

Sparrow heard Puckel's mention of the dragon's dream, but it was not until much later that he remembered it again. Too many questions were crowding into his head. "What happens to your shape?" he whispered.

Puckel screwed up his eyes. "Let it be enough for you to know that it disappears so that it's there for you to return to," he said. "If everyone could see it when you were out of it, it wouldn't be your own any more."

Sparrow scarcely heard. Another question had already occurred to him. "What about people?" he said. "Can you change into another person?"

Puckel was silent for a moment, before saying one word, so softly that Sparrow could hardly hear above the hiss of a stick in the fire. "Yes." And Sparrow felt a cold fear inside him, for as Puckel said it, all the old man's inner laughter suddenly disappeared.

"I don't want you to change into me," Sparrow said quickly.

"I won't," Puckel replied quietly. "And no

shape-shifter who is wise should ever change into another person – and nor should you, when you have the power."

"I won't," said Sparrow. He had forgotten for the moment that it was Bull who had asked for this wish.

"Do you want this wish?" Puckel asked. "They are your wishes and you can have them for yourself."

Then Sparrow remembered. With an effort, sadly, he said, "No, I'd better not. I said I would get the wishes for Bull and Gogs – that's what I told them."

"You could fly back to them," said Puckel, "and tell them you'd changed your mind and taken your wishes for yourself."

"I could fly back to them and tell them you couldn't give my wishes to them, only to me," Sparrow suggested.

"No, you couldn't," said Puckel, "because it wouldn't be true, and that's a fact. And we do not tell lies."

Sparrow felt quite scared he had even thought of telling a lie.

"If you want the wishes for yourself, that is what you must tell your friends," said Puckel.

Sparrow considered. He would have loved to have the power of shape-changing, but he had not forgotten how being able to fly had made him feel so different from the others. What would it be like if he was the only one who could understand beasts and birds, and the only one who could shape-change? It might be good, but it would be terribly lonely, maybe even too lonely to bear... On the other hand, it would be something that Bull didn't have. Bull could keep his secrets and his gran's stories. Perhaps he would let Gogs have his wish and take Bull's for himself...

"No," he said at last with an effort, "I want Gogs and Bull to have magic powers too."

"Then make a wish for each of them to fly like you," said Puckel, "and then you'll all be the same."

"Could I tell them those were the only wishes you'd give me?" asked Sparrow doubtfully.

"No, you couldn't," Puckel answered sternly.

Sparrow sighed. "Then I'll just have to ask you for the things they told me to ask you for."

Puckel said, "I can grant you these wishes, though I don't want to do it. I must if you ask me, because I promised you."

"Bull and Gogs are my friends," Sparrow explained, "and I want to be able to do things with them."

"Then you must have what you ask," said Puckel. "Now you are like a glass of clear water, little Sparrow," – his voice sounded quite sad – "and your friend can look straight through you. In the end it will be a good thing."

"And now," he continued, "are you listening?" Puckel's wild old eyebrows were drawn close together – he was frowning, and his green eyes seemed to shoot out dangerous little tongues of fire.

"Yes," said Sparrow.

"Then come on, come on, come here and look."

He sounded impatient, so Sparrow jumped up from the chair by the fire and went over to where Puckel was looking into the bowl of water on the table.

Sparrow did as he was told, and there, clear and small, like a perfect little picture in a book – but moving and alive – he saw the trees round the clearing he had left less than two hours earlier, and Bull and Gogs wandering about, looking bored and a little annoyed. It was so real he felt he could have reached into the bowl and touched them.

"Now," whispered Puckel, "tell them that they have their wishes."

"Bull," began Sparrow – but in the moment he spoke, the water in the bowl became rippled and ruffled. Sparrow could still see Gogs and Bull, but they were pulled out of shape by the twisting water, so that it looked as if two small black monsters were wandering about in a jungle of nightmare.

"Go on," whispered Puckel. "Tell them."

"Bull, you'll be able to change your shape," said Sparrow, "and understand beasts and birds, and Gogs will be able to understand beasts and birds and fly." And as he spoke, the little figures of Bull and Gogs twisted and jumped and danced in the writhing forest, till it looked as though they were being torn into pieces and thrown up among the branches of the trees. He watched, horrified, but as soon as he had finished speaking, the water calmed down and the picture became clear and still again. There were Gogs and Bull standing in the clearing, but now they were looking about them with strange expressions on their faces.

Puckel said, "When you watched them without speaking, the picture was clear. That was because you were doing only one thing. When you watched and spoke, the picture was pulled out of shape: that was because you were doing two things. Your friends each asked for two things as if they were one. They will have those two things, to be sure they will have them: they will not be half-gifts. But nothing will turn out as clear or as straight for them as if they had only asked for one. Remember this, young Sparrow."

"All right," said Sparrow.

"Then off you go now, and when you need me, call me and you'll find me."

Puckel passed his hand over the bowl, and the water in it shot up into the air like a fountain. Just before it hit the ceiling, it arched over and came twisting down in a spiral, not at all like water. For a moment, Sparrow caught a glimpse of the snake in that curling, coiling water, before suddenly, brown and hard and shiny, there it was again – a twisted stick in the old man's hand.

This time Sparrow didn't fly up into the air, or at least he didn't remember doing it. Puckel, his stick, the cave, the bowl, the table, the chair and the fire, all simply disappeared and Sparrow was left floating in the air, high above the mountain tops.

He felt strange and – even though he was floating – heavy and so tired. He floated more than he flew, rocking down like a leaf from the mountains over the forest, softly and slowly back to the clearing he had left with such high hopes.

He landed, stopped, and looked around. The clearing was empty. Gogs and Bull had gone.

Sparrow walked home. The tiredness would not pass and he went to bed early, and slept and slept, right through till lunchtime the next day. It was such a deep, black sleep that it was like being buried in the earth; and when he woke up again, he could hardly remember who he was or where he was or what day it was.

Slowly things began to come back to him: the events of the day before; Puckel; Bull and Gogs getting their wishes. He had better get up and go and see if he could find his friends.

But on the way down the path, Sparrow met a boy coming up from the village with a message: Ms Minn was back, and school was to open again the next day. Sparrow turned back and went to tell Murie.

It was a windy, sunny day, and Murie decided then and there to wash all Sparrow's clothes so that he would have something clean to wear to school. Sparrow had to take everything off, and went about for the rest of the day in a warm old shirt which had belonged to his father. It was so long it came down past his knees, and although it was comfortable enough he felt embarrassed about going off to find Bull and Gogs dressed like that.

He spent the day wondering why his friends hadn't waited for him, and whether they really had received their gifts and were going about flying or listening to what the beasts and birds said.

When he thought about this, he began to feel a little miserable – he realized properly for the first time that the gifts of Gogs and Bull were much more than his own.

That night Sparrow dreamed he saw an aeroplane. It was just as he had imagined it would be – a tube with stiff wings sticking out at the sides – and he felt delighted. Then it was right up close to him and he was standing on one of the great flat wings, tipping backwards and forwards on it to keep his balance, and bending down to peer inside the windows that ran all along the tube.

Sure enough, there seemed to be people inside it, but Sparrow was only able to make out one, and that was Ms Minn. She was sitting in the very front, hanging on to a set of horse's reins and apparently steering the aeroplane with them. The wind was blowing her hair about, and with a far-away, foolish expression on her face she was chanting the words, "At the third stone, the time has come! At the third stone, the time has come!" over and over.

At that moment, Sparrow felt himself slipping. He wrapped his arms round the wing of the aeroplane and looked down: down, down, to empty air beneath him – nothing but empty air, and far, far away, a dark splodge that could have been the earth. And a horror grew in him that he could no longer fly...

When he woke he was trembling and sweating. But it was morning and time to get up for school.

His dream had seemed so real that Sparrow felt certain he had lost the power of flight. On the way down the path from the house, he glanced round to make sure he was alone, then jumped and – oh, the relief! – yes, he could still fly. He dropped down a bit, and skimmed on just above the road. A little further on and then

I'll walk, he was thinking, when – *slam!* Something caught him hard between the shoulders and sent him staggering forwards, landing and tripping on the hard road. He came down on to his knees – not too hard, but just hard enough to make him feel annoyed.

He looked behind him. There was Gogs, hovering a little above the ground and grinning all over his freckly face.

Now Sparrow felt really annoyed. "Where were you?" he shouted crossly. "Why didn't you come and see me?"

Gogs stopped grinning. "I was coming up to see you just now. Then I heard a bird saying you were flying down the path, so I thought I'd hide and surprise you. I couldn't come before, because all my clothes were getting washed. So were Bull's. It didn't stop Bull though. He turned into a bird and came across to tell me, though when he turned back into Bull he didn't have any clothes on!" Gogs laughed.

"Why didn't Bull come to see me? Why did he just go to you?" Sparrow said.

Gogs shrugged. "I wished I'd asked to be a shape-shifter too," he went on, "but Bull says that when you turn into something else you can't see things properly and you can't think properly, so maybe it's better fun just being able to fly."

"What's it like hearing the beasts and birds?"

Sparrow asked. He was curious, even though he did still feel cross.

"It's confusing," said Gogs, "because you hear these voices going on all round you, big ones and little ones and high ones and low ones. But Bull told me you can make it go quiet if you think about it, and you can. I don't hear anything talking just now, but if I wanted to listen I could."

"What's that bird saying?" Sparrow asked, pointing to a chaffinch in the bare elm tree across the road. It was chuff-chuffing to itself in a contented fashion.

Gogs listened. "Nothing very interesting," he said. "Just something about some barley spilled down at the mill. I think it's swelling up inside him. He says he feels like a stuffed turkey."

Sparrow giggled, though inside him something was regretting, regretting. Why had he let Gogs and Bull have his wishes? Gogs didn't even seem particularly interested in his. If I'd got the gift of understanding beasts and birds, Sparrow thought to himself, I wouldn't make it go quiet: I'd listen to everything, for days and days...

Bull appeared on the road ahead. He might have been walking down from his house, but Sparrow suspected he had been shape-shifting.

Bull's brooding face looked unusually pleased. "You should see what we can do," he said. "I can do just about anything now."

Sparrow immediately felt that something was not right about Bull. Or had Bull always been like this and Sparrow just hadn't thought about it properly? A new wave of anger swept over him. Bull hadn't so much as thanked him! Yet mixed with the anger there was that fear again. Only now he understood at last what he was scared of: he was plain scared of Bull. Had he always been, or had it only become real fear now that Bull had this awesome power? He swallowed his thoughts, and said, "We'll have to hurry. We'll be late for school."

"Huh! School!" said Bull scornfully. "Why go to school when you can do what we can do? You don't learn anything at school!"

Gogs looked horrified. "Oh, we've got to go to school," he said. "Everyone does that."

"Who could make us?" said Bull. "They couldn't make us stay in the classroom, and they couldn't even catch us if we decided to fly away. Or I could turn into a brick or a tree or something and they'd never even know I was there. Or I could even turn into Ms Minn herself, and then I would know everything that she knows and I could be your teacher – and I could easily just shut the school up and say there'd be a holiday for as long as we wanted."

"You wouldn't really do that, would you?" asked Sparrow. "P — the old man told me you shouldn't shift into other people's shapes, you know."

Two Things...

"Well, he never told me that," said Bull unconcernedly. "Anyway, I tried it with my gran last night when she was knitting. She just thought she'd been knitting in her sleep. She found she'd knitted a whole sock without even knowing! 'I knew I was good,' she said, 'but I didn't know I was that good!' I didn't tell her I'd been doing it for her!"

If Bull changed into his gran, Sparrow thought, does that mean he knows everything that she does? Is that why he's different? Then a worse thought struck him. Was that why Bull had said Sparrow and Gogs wouldn't leave him behind when they were flying – because he would simply change into one of them? The thought horrified him. "Aren't you going to school today then?" he asked tensely.

"I'm going for one day," Bull announced. "I'm going to ask Ms Minn one question – I'm going to ask if she can teach us anything real."

"What do you mean, *real*?" said Sparrow.

"What do we do all day at school?" said Bull with a scornful twist to his mouth. "Sit all day and add up numbers – what for? And why do we have to fiddle about with calculators when we do it? What difference does that make?"

Gogs looked worried, but Sparrow shrugged. "Why do you have to know why you're doing it?" he said. "It's just what you do."

67

"Well, it's not good enough for me," said Bull. "Not any more. So I'm going to ask her. And if she can't tell me, I'm going to turn into her, and that way I'll find out if she really does know anything or not – and then I'm going to go away, or if I feel like it I might come back and teach you all some of the things I know."

They went on in silence, Sparrow and Gogs walking a little ahead of Bull.

Ms Minn hadn't changed a bit. She was wispy and wild and vague as ever; she was dressed in the same dusty old black clothes, and she talked in just the same way. Everyone was very quiet, and she made them press the buttons on their calculators all through the morning while they did money-counting sums in their heads.

Sparrow glanced over at Bull a few times, but he seemed to be thinking very hard about something, and not noticing anything that was going on. He was certainly not pressing his calculator buttons.

But after lunch, Ms Minn announced in her dry, scrapy voice, "Now children, this afternoon I'm going to test you to see if you remember how to address a Prospective Employer. Bull, will you come forward, please? You are the interviewee for the job of advertising agent, and I am the interviewer."

Bull stood up, but he didn't come forward.

Two Things...

He folded his arms across his chest, looked Ms Minn straight in the eye, and said, "Ms Minn, could you teach us something real, for a change?"

BULL AND THE
DRAGON

The silence that followed Bull's question was the quietest, most breathless silence imaginable. You could have heard the mice squeaking behind the walls, only they had fallen silent too. You would have thought the little black beetle crawling across the floor would have gone on tiptoe. No one had ever spoken in that way to Ms Minn before.

But for all her strangeness, Ms Minn was not easily surprised. She stood quietly, clasping her hands together as she always did, and looked straight at Bull with her frail old head on one side, like a thrush about to spear a worm.

"Very well, my dear," she said. "What would you like to know?"

Bull was not flustered. "Well, you want us to speak to a Prospective Employer," he began.

"Yes, of course," Ms Minn put in.

"But we don't even know what a Prospective Employer is!"

"But you know how to talk to him," Ms Minn said quietly.

"What's the use of that," said Bull, "if we never meet one?"

"No use at all," said Ms Minn.

"Well, that's just what I mean," said Bull angrily. "You don't teach us real things. You make us press buttons on calculators – but what do the calculators do?"

"Nothing, I don't think," Ms Minn answered simply.

"That's what I mean," said Bull. "So what is a calculator? What's it made for? Who made it? Why did we sit and press buttons on calculators all morning? You make us sit and count money, but what's money? What's it for?"

"Nothing," said Ms Minn again.

"Well, why's it here?" said Bull. "Where does it come from? Who made it? Why did they make it? Those are the things I want to learn."

Ms Minn straightened up. And something about her seemed to change, almost as though someone inside her had suddenly woken up – someone who had been hiding behind Ms Minn's sometimes foolish exterior, waiting for years for this moment to arrive.

"Then I shall teach you the things you want to learn," she said in her quiet, dry voice. "I shall tell you a story. About a dragon."

"Is this a fairy story?" Bull demanded.

71

Jet Smoke and Dragon Fire

A whisper of confusion ran round the class. Apart from Sparrow and Gogs, no one in the class even knew what a real fairy story was. For that matter, no one knew what a dragon was, any more than they knew what a Prospective Employer was, or an advertising agent.

"This story," Ms Minn said – and her voice became as quiet and as cold as ice creeping across a pool of water – "this story is everything. It is a fairy story and a true story, a history and a mystery."

"Long, long ago," Ms Minn began, "a dragon came down from the mountains. The dragon was full of marvellous ideas, and was always thinking of wonderful things to make. And it would have made them, but it couldn't because it was only a dragon. I think that may have been why it left its home.

"As soon as it came to live among people, it started giving them the ideas for all the things it had dreamed up. It was the dragon, long ago, who dreamed up all the odd things we see around us but have no use for: the calculators, the televisions, the telephones, the glass light-bulbs that hang in our houses, the railway lines and the roads that disappear in the distance.

"Why we don't use them will be explained in due course, Bull, so you don't need to interrupt. There were other things, too, that most

72

of you won't have heard about. I can't tell you about them all, because there is no time – but I can tell you that the dragon thought particularly about things which would take a lot of people quickly from one place to another. There were boats as big as villages to travel on the water, strings of waggons like giant snakes that rushed along the railway lines, and shining tubes that people could sit inside and fly through the air in –"

Sparrow looked triumphantly over at Bull, but Bull seemed to be sunk deep in thought again.

"The televisions, the telephones, the lights and the calculators," Ms Minn went on, " had the same kind of purpose, because all the things the dragon dreamed up were things which made people think about what was far-off and forget about what was close at hand. There were little windows in which people could see what was far away, horns into which they could speak to people who were far away, little boxes to keep their memory in so they didn't have to keep it in their heads, lights that turned night into day because the people liked to sleep through half the daylight.

"All the things the dragon invented may seem magical to you, but they were not. For though the dragon is a magical beast, when its ideas are made into things, their magic goes: they were just machines, just ordinary things like spades and cups and millwheels. And the dragon did not like this, for a magical beast likes only magical things. So the dragon became unsatisfied and restless, and often angry. It was its own fault, because it should have stayed in the mountains, but knowing that didn't help its temper at all.

"The dragon, you see, is not supposed to live where living creatures live, because its breath is poisonous. When it breathes, smoke comes out of its nose and mouth, and if people or animals or even plants and trees breathe in the smoke, they become very sick. The animals and trees and plants just die when they get sick, but people who breathe the dragon-breath go mad.

"The people built a city round the place where the dragon lived. A city is like a thousand villages all built together, and because there were so many buildings and so many people, there wasn't room for animals and plants: no one noticed that everything died when it came near the dragon. But of course all the people went mad. Only they went mad so slowly that no one noticed.

"As I told you, the dragon became angry when it saw that none of the things the people made were actually magical. So it began to dream up machines that would destroy all the wonderful things it had invented. And by now the people were so mad that they were quite happy to make these machines and to use them. In this way, whole cities were destroyed, and even whole countries, and the dragon would join in the destruction and fly over the land bellowing and blasting out flames and smoke. Thousands upon thousands of people were killed, but those left simply buried their dead and forgot about them and went on with the work of making and destroying. You must not forget how mad the dragon's breath had made them.

"But the dragon itself was not mad – just very angry – and at last it flew off to find somewhere to cool down before it burst with rage.

"The place it chose was a lonely part of the world where there was a great lake. It plunged into this, and the water bubbled and boiled, and mist and steam rose up and covered the land all around, and where the mist and steam settled everything died. There the dragon stayed for a long time, making itself cool and hiding from the people.

"Not far from the lake, up in the mountains, there lived an old man. He wasn't like other men. For one thing he was much, much older, and for another he didn't go mad with the dragon's breath. He would go down to the side of the lake and speak to the dragon, for days, weeks, months at a time. The dragon wouldn't agree to go back to its own place, but it did stop being so angry – it was a lot cooler with the water by now – and it began to trust the old man.

"At last the old man said to the dragon, 'You can't stay in the lake all the time. Your skin will go wrinkly and soft and before you know it you'll be nothing but a wriggling, slimy worm. Follow me and I'll show you a place where you can hide and no one will find you.'

"The dragon agreed, and one dark night it came out of the lake and followed the old man up into the mountains. The old man walked slowly along a quiet railway line, with the dragon creeping along behind him like a gigantic white lizard. It was white because of the water: normally it was green and golden. At last they came to a place where the line went into a tunnel that cut right through one of the biggest mountains. The line led to a city hundreds of kilometres in the distance, but the old man didn't intend to take the dragon there. He waited until they were in the deepest and darkest part of the tunnel, and then suddenly he ran on ahead, so softly and quickly that the dragon didn't hear him going. But when the old man had got far enough through the tunnel, he let out a shout. It was such a terrible, long, deafening shout that the roof of the tunnel cracked, and the whole mountain slipped. The tunnel was completely blocked at one end, and the dragon was trapped in the ruins. To be quite accurate, it wasn't really trapped. The tunnel was still open behind it. But you must realize that the dragon was very long, and fitted closely into the tunnel, so that it couldn't turn round. And although the dragon is very magical, there isn't a part of it that would ever think of going backwards. So there the dragon stayed.

"The old man ran on, almost to the end of the mountains, but long before the city was in sight he turned and shouted again. And the shout that he gave then echoed from mountain to mountain, till rocks and boulders started breaking off from the tall stony peaks, and came bouncing and spinning down in a deafening, crashing shower that shook the ground and made underground waters spout and hiss up through cracks. By the time the din had stopped and the waters had settled down again, the rocks that had shaken loose from the mountains were half filling the valleys in great ruinous heaps, and the railway line was completely hidden from sight.

"Meanwhile, in the tunnel, the dragon was snorting and bellowing with rage at the trick the old man had played on it, but because of the disturbance in the mountains all the fumes and smoke it snorted found their way through vents and fissures under the ground and rose up in a wall of cloud all around the mountains where the dragon was trapped.

This dragon-mist, like the dragon's breath, was poisonous, but now, after seeping under the ground, it didn't exactly make people go mad: it just made it impossible for them to see things properly. So no one from the world outside was able to find where the dragon was: the dragon-mist made the mountains seem invisible, or at most like great white clouds heaped on the horizon. The people from the world outside simply stopped using the railway line that led nowhere, and gradually forgot about it. They were still quite mad, poor things, and forgot very easily. And the people in the five mountain villages forgot about the world outside.

"And now the dragon sleeps beneath the mountain where it was trapped. But as it sleeps it dreams, and everything that happens in the world passes through its mind. And sometimes, very occasionally, someone will stop and think he is living inside the dragon's dream; and when that happens it means that the time has come when — "

Suddenly Ms Minn stopped and frowned. "Bull," she said quietly, "are you listening?"

Ms Minn's words were just beginning to stir something in Sparrow's memory, but what happened next made him forget what it was until a good deal later. Everyone looked over at Bull, but Bull didn't seem to notice. He was sitting at his desk, with his hands hanging over the front of it and his head drooping till it was almost resting on his arms. Sparrow thought his eyes were not quite closed, but he looked very much as though he were asleep.

Bull still did not stir or answer. Ms Minn went over to him. She stood beside him a moment, and then she put her hand on his head. "Bull, you're cold," she said.

She put her hand under Bull's chin and raised his head. Then one of the girls screamed. Sparrow saw that Bull's eyes were open, but they were rolling, and you could see only the whites under his lids. Steadily, the hair of Bull's head lifted until it was all standing up on end. The girl screamed again. One boy whimpered and others were shifting uneasily in their seats. But a second later the whole class became utterly silent.

Ms Minn's hand was still under Bull's chin, but now, as she raised his head up, the whole of Bull's body rose from his seat. As his legs came up, he knocked over his desk with a crash.

"Goodness," said Ms Minn. Bull was in a position as if still sitting at his desk, but he was floating a metre from the ground. Ms Minn let go of his chin. Bull remained up in the air.

Very slowly, Ms Minn stepped back. One step, then another. Bull floated after her. She stepped back again, never taking her eyes off him, until she had retreated as far as she could go, and her back was against the blackboard at the top end of the classroom. Bull floated slowly, steadily towards her, as though he were in an invisible flying chair.

Just in front of Ms Minn's nose, he stopped. He hung there, completely without moving, for as long as it would take you to count to ten quite slowly.

Then he began to float backwards. At the far end of the classroom there was a large, high window, and towards this he travelled with gathering speed. Through the window's polished glass you could see the mountains climbing, one behind the other, to the heights where the first snow had already fallen. Faster and faster Bull went now, backwards, straight towards the window.

"Ms Minn! Please! Stop him!" the girl screamed again. Bull was hurtling backwards now, his dark hair lashing wildly on either side of his face. The classroom seemed to have got longer, to have stretched out like a tunnel, because still Bull went flying giddily, as fast as a stone dropped over the edge of a cliff. A whining, buzzing noise filled the air and one by one the children clapped their hands over their ears to keep the noise out. Soon it was almost unbearable, even with their ears covered. And still Bull hurtled backwards. Dimly they saw Ms Minn standing with her back to the blackboard. The blackboard seemed to have got smaller, or else she had suddenly grown. Quiet and calm and tall, she stood there looking at Bull, while the horrible air buzzed and whined about her…

And then – *smash!* and straight afterwards *crash!* and then an icy tinkling as the broken glass showered down the classroom wall on to the floor. The air cleared immediately, and the whining stopped. The classroom shrank back to its proper size. So did Ms Minn. Bull had disappeared, and only a gaping hole in the window showed where he had gone.

Like a flight of starlings leaving a tree, everyone leaped up and ran to the sill.

Bull was far away up the street that led to the middle of the village, sitting on his bottom as though he had just landed. He was looking more normal now, gazing about him as if he were wondering how he came to be there in the middle of the road. He didn't seem to have been injured by the glass, and in fact the glass looked more as though it had shattered and fallen out of the pane before Bull hit it: it was all lying in a heap on the classroom floor, and there seemed to be none on the ground out-side. One of the doors of the houses out on the street opened, and a fat woman came out and looked at Bull, wiping her hands on a cloth. But the moment he saw the faces appearing at the schoolroom window, Bull did a backward somersault, leaped to his feet, and rushed off up the street through the village and up towards the mountains like a mad rabbit.

"Goodness me," Ms Minn said again. "Oh dear. Oh dear, oh dear, I must see my brother. Oh dear, that's possibly it then, isn't it?" She turned round, went to the classroom door and opened it. As she went through, "That's all, dears," she said absently. "School's over."

And school really was over, after only one day. Such a thing had never happened before, and in fact none of them ever had Ms Minn as a teacher again. But it was quite a long time before the village people realized that she would never come back.

"What do you think happened?" Sparrow muttered to Gogs as soon as he got the chance.

"I don't know," Gogs whispered back. He looked scared.

"Come on," said Sparrow, and they slipped through the commotion of excited children and left the school.

Before long they saw Ms Minn striding across the village square ahead of them. "We'll have to tell her," said Gogs.

"Tell her what?"

"Tell her we know what's happened."

"But we don't!" Sparrow exclaimed.

"Well, he must have shifted shape or something…" Gogs tailed off.

"He didn't shift shape, did he?" said Sparrow. "Something else happened."

"Well, we should tell her it's because of magic, anyway," Gogs insisted.

"What was that she was muttering about her brother?" Sparrow said. "Who's her brother?"

Gogs shrugged. "Come on," he said, "or we'll never catch her up."

They ran, but even so the old lady was going at such a rate that they didn't begin to catch up with her until they were under the bare elms on the street that led up from the village on to the Old Road.

"Ms Minn!" Gogs panted as she flapped on ahead of them. "Ms Minn!" But there seemed to be a wind blowing here – almost as though it were blowing round Ms Minn because she was walking so fast – and she appeared not to hear him.

"Ms Minn!" Gogs called a third time. Suddenly Sparrow gave an exclamation, stopped, and bent down to pick something off the road. With his eyes fixed on the old teacher, he had seen something drop from the ragged edge of her black dress – something that gleamed in a quite unmistakable way...

Gogs stopped and turned back to look at what he had found. Sparrow was gaping in disbelief at the thing he was holding in his hand: a milkstone.

"It fell from her clothes," Sparrow said, as

both boys stared down at it. "I saw it falling. It came from her."

It was a perfect stone. Smooth, round, flawless, like a milky gleaming egg, its two layers of gold flake forming two perfect rings round its surface. "We'd better give it back to her," Gogs breathed.

But when they looked again, there was no sign of Ms Minn, either on the cobbled road or up on the Old Road. She had simply disappeared.

"I want to see P —" Sparrow stopped and frowned. "The old man," he finished. "I don't know what's going on." Vaguely, deep inside him, he did know, but his mind was racing too much for him to stop and think.

"I'll come too," Gogs said. "I'd like to practise my flying anyway." And as soon as they had reached the Old Road they flew.

Within moments, Gogs had forgotten all about Bull in the sheer delight of flying. Sparrow was more used to it, so he didn't forget, and Gogs was content to follow him. They flew over the forest, over the Cliff of Stones and down to the waterfall. Here Sparrow landed. He did not intend to waste time again trying to find the old man's cave by flying. He came to the foot of the little dark stream and started labouring up the hillside on foot, following its course.

"Come on," Gogs urged when they had reached the ash wood. "Fly!"

"No use," Sparrow panted, "we won't find it."

"Why?" Gogs demanded.

"I don't know," Sparrow puffed, "we just won't."

"That's stupid," Gogs scoffed. "We'd be quicker if we flew."

"I'm walking," Sparrow replied, "it's the only way to get there."

"Where is old Piddle's cave?" Gogs asked.

"Up at the top of the stream," Sparrow answered, "but you've got to keep near the water."

"I know what," said Gogs. "I'll fly on ahead, and if I get lost, I'll ask the birds. They're bound to know."

"All right," said Sparrow. But the idea still did not tempt him to fly.

Sparrow watched Gogs skimming away over the stream amongst the trees. But long before he was out of sight between the straight grey trunks, Sparrow saw him land, scratch his head, look about and seem to speak. Sparrow guessed he was asking the birds, having somehow lost sight of the little dark stream. What he didn't know was that when Gogs asked the birds, the air all around filled with chirping and cheeping, but all Gogs could understand was, "Pickle, piddle, prickle, puddle, puckle, poker, kittle, cuddle, fiddle, fuddle, flimsy, mimsy, poodle, strudel, tickle, tuckle," and so on and on. Sparrow saw Gogs rise into the air again – higher this time, and higher again, until he lost sight of him in the lacing branches of the forest trees. He toiled on, keeping close to the little dark stream. A quarter of an hour passed, a stitch crept into his side and his breath was rough in his throat, but still he kept up the steepening slope. The milkstone in his hand felt greasy with sweat.

"Ow!" Sparrow suddenly yelled out loud. Something like a blow to his back jolted him from head to foot and brought him to a stand-still. What on earth was wrong? He found he had started trembling all over, and his legs wouldn't hold him. Gradually his knees gave way and he slipped down the bank into the little dark stream.

Cold water round his lower half revived him, but whatever it was that had jolted him had also left a thought in his head. Something he had not even started to consider in all the excitement of the last half hour...

Ms Minn's story was about their own mountains – their own railway line, the dead lake – the tunnel!

And the dragon in the tunnnel? Well, what about the dragon...? Sparrow had no wish to meet any dragon, head-first or tail-first, and yet his curiosity was gnawing him. Suppose he went down to the tunnel now and looked – not far, but just a little way in – just to check if Ms Minn's story really ended in that particular tunnel; just to check if the story was really true. It was strange how urgent that thought became in his mind, because he knew that the sensible thing to do just now was to go on and find Puckel and ask about Bull. And yet the thought of climbing up another kilometre of steep mountainside did not seem very inviting – and how did he know that Puckel would even be there at the end of it?

He pulled himself out of the water and squelched up the bank. He didn't feel like making decisions: he was wet, and he wanted to fly and he wanted to have a quick look at the tunnel. He rose through the trees. High up and higher he went, until he could see all that part of the mountain region spreading out beneath him: the white-capped peaks, the dark, greyish forests, the village far below with its blue haze of smoke, the old railway line climbing and winding up from the village, disappearing behind a rocky mound, appearing again, higher all the time.

There was a small dark figure wandering along the railway track. Sparrow didn't waste a second: he plunged straight down towards it like a falcon, and within seconds was landing in a small shower of water on the track behind the figure. It was Gogs again.

"Gogs," he called, "have you seen Bull?"

Slowly Gogs turned and looked at Sparrow. Sparrow stopped and frowned. There was something wrong with Gogs – Sparrow couldn't quite put his finger on it. It was something about the way Gogs turned and stared at him that wasn't like Gogs. For an instant it actually reminded him of Bull. Gogs waited for Sparrow to catch up with him. "What's wrong?" Sparrow asked anxiously.

"Bull's dead," Gogs said, almost in a whisper. He half glanced at Sparrow, then looked down at his feet.

Again, just for an instant, just before he thought about what Gogs had said, Sparrow thought there was something wrong with Gogs' voice; something wrong with the way he wouldn't look straight at him. Next moment he took in the meaning of Gogs' words and forgot all about his strangeness.

"Dead?" he echoed. "How can he be dead? He was at school this afternoon."

AT THE THIRD STONE

"He fell over a cliff," Gogs answered in the same level, quiet voice. "He was running along the steep path, and he must have slipped. All the birds were talking about it, so I came to see."

Sparrow looked hard at Gogs. "Where is he?" Sparrow said. "And where are you going?"

"I –" again Gogs looked up in that strange, half-glancing way at Sparrow, and looked away again "– I was just coming to see if I could find you."

"Why didn't you fly then?" Sparrow demanded.

"I forgot," Gogs replied promptly. "I was too upset."

"Where is he?" Sparrow asked again.

"That way," said Gogs, pointing back down the railway line.

"Did you fly down to him?" Sparrow enquired.

Gogs remained looking at his feet. He shook his head. "I was scared to," he muttered.

Sparrow felt his own legs going wobbly. He remembered his dream of the night before. "Come on," he said. "Show me the place."

They walked back down the track in silence, stepping from sleeper to sleeper. Everything around them was quiet. They came to a place where a path led down from the railway line and Gogs took this path until it levelled out near the edge of the cliff. Then he stopped and pointed down.

For a moment Sparrow could see only rocks: huge boulders, smaller stones, all tumbled together in a long grey scree at the cliff's foot. Then he saw the tiny, sprawled-out human figure. He could not make out properly what the figure was wearing, but somehow he knew it was Bull.

He had been going to say to Gogs that they should fly down to him and perhaps carry him back up. But he couldn't bring himself to do it. Looking down there, he simply felt scared. Sparrow, who had flown so high above the mountain tops that he could hardly breathe for the thinness of the air, looked down that hundred metre cliff and was sure that if he jumped he would end up the same way as Bull – smashed over a rock. He felt dizzy and sick.

Then – "Something's moving," he said, peering down.

"I can't see anything," Gogs said.

"Maybe not," Sparrow mumbled. "I thought I could see something moving."

"Bull won't move again," Gogs said with a catch in his voice as though he were fighting back tears.

Sparrow felt his own throat knotting up. "We'll have to tell someone," he said thickly.

"Have you seen the old man?" Gogs asked.

"No," said Sparrow, without explaining why.

"You go and see him," said Gogs, "and I'll fly back to the village and tell someone."

Sparrow agreed to this, and on the railway track they parted, Gogs flying back down the hill while Sparrow left the track and made off again in the direction of Puckel's cave.

Sparrow was still shaking with the shock and he made sure he didn't do any high flying, skimming instead. But he was not used to flying through the mountains this way, and soon he came to a ridge where he landed and looked around, uncertain of his direction.

The land here was a tumble of forest, gullies and ridges, and glancing back the way he had come, Sparrow saw a part of the railway line again between the folds of rocky ground. And at that very moment, he saw a figure on the track – or rather not quite on the track: surely it was flying above the track...

It must be Gogs again, Sparrow thought – and then he frowned. For Gogs was going back the way he had come: not down towards the village but up, in the direction he had been going when Sparrow first found him – into the mountains.

Towards the tunnel. And as the thought struck him, again there came that over-whelming urge – forgotten because of the shock of Bull's death – to go and investigate the tunnel. For the second time, Sparrow was on the point of abandoning his search for Puckel to go back there, to follow the track into the dark, deeper and deeper into the heart of the mountain – where, in the mountain's heart, surrounded by its poisonous smoky breath that made you go mad, the terrible, wise, magical dragon lay stuck, trapped with its tail stretching back towards the open air!

Trapped. And by whom? Of course: by the old man who wasn't like other men. He had to be – Puckel!

Sparrow span round like a top. He had to get to Puckel! But then there was the dragon in the tunnel. Vividly he imagined the fearful beast, and Gogs tiptoeing over the sleepers towards it, closer, closer...

The dragon, Puckel. Puckel, the dragon. They both seemed to pull at him, dragging him this way and that as though he were the bone in a dogs' tug-of-war.

In the end, Puckel proved the stronger thought. But it was hard: hard as getting out of your warm bed early on a cold winter morning. Sparrow managed to decide, but only just: whatever Gogs was doing, the only way of getting help was to get Puckel.

He reached the little dark stream again and ran, ran and ran, till his chest was heaving and painful and his breath tasted of blood. His legs, already chilled from their wetting, seemed too heavy to move, till gradually all the feeling drained out of them – and still he ran, automatically, and barely noticed it when he at last pushed through the close, cooling leaves of the ivy. There in the courtyard of rocks stood Puckel, and Sparrow collapsed at his feet where the little dark stream bubbled up through the stones.

"Puckel," he gasped. "Bull's fallen off the cliff – he's dead – and Ms Minn dropped a milk-stone and she's off again; something happened with Bull and she's off to see … and Gogs isn't going down to the village and I think there's something wrong with him too, and I got this bang in the back and my legs got wet and —"

Puckel held up his hand, and Sparrow found his mouth clapping shut. The next thing he knew was that he was half lying in Puckel's chair by the fire, and Puckel was sitting cross-legged on the table staring intently into the brown bowl. Dully Sparrow's eyes moved round the room in the cave. There was no sign of the stick or the snake, so he assumed that Puckel had turned it into the water for the bowl again.

At last the old man looked up, nodding solemnly. "Yes," he remarked, "it's bad: it's very bad, it's very, very bad indeed."

"I know it is," Sparrow said, "that's what I was trying to tell you. Bull's dead." And then his chest heaved, once, twice, and tears overwhelmed him.

"Hush," said Puckel, after Sparrow had quietened a little. "His body – his body is all broken, although it is already quickly mending. That is being attended to, as you'd have noticed if you had sharper eyes. But Bull's not dead."

"You mean we can still help him?" Sparrow gulped.

"Not in the way you think," Puckel replied briskly. "What you saw, below the cliff, is beyond your help. But Bull is not dead. You saw Bull."

"I know," Sparrow answered, rubbing his eyes feverishly, "he had fallen over the cliff."

"You saw Bull," Puckel repeated impatiently. "You saw him, and spoke to him, and you didn't see who he was."

"But I did," Sparrow protested, "I mean – the only person I spoke to was Gogs."

"You spoke to Bull," Puckel insisted.

94

Sparrow gave one last almighty sniff. "I don't know what you can see in that bowl," he said rudely, "but I think you must be disturbing the water. Gogs is the one with red hair —"

"I know, I know," Puckel interrupted, "the red hair and the idiot's grin. I saw him before. This bowl, boy, doesn't show me pictures – it's not a silly circus trick that you do with a stick and a slop of water." He held the bowl up and turned it towards Sparrow, who saw that it was quite empty – a dry, rough earthenware hollow. "It tells me things in here," Puckel said, tapping his head. "I don't make mistakes from seeing what isn't there. You spoke to Bull, not Gogs."

"You mean Bull turned into Gogs?" Sparrow gasped. Of course: Gogs had been so strange. "But then what – why could we still see Bull's body? It should have disappeared."

"When someone dies suddenly," Puckel said, "it can sometimes take a little time for them to realize they're dead. And of course someone who doesn't realize he's dead isn't properly dead. That has saved Bull. He should have died when he fell, but in the brief time given to him, he saw Gogs looking over the cliff at his body below – and he took Gogs' shape. It was lucky and it was very close. But the thread that held him to his body had already been broken, so when he took Gogs' shape he had to leave his own body behind."

"Can't he get it back?" Sparrow asked.

"We shall see," said Puckel. "There's a good chance of it. But Bull has been very foolish – as I expected him to be. Don't say I didn't warn you."

Sparrow was silent.

"I'll tell you what I read," Puckel said. "The teacher in the classroom –" He paused.

"You mean Ms Minn," Sparrow said.

Puckel grunted, a grunt that was nearly a chuckle. "Ms Minn," he repeated. "Well, she told her story. Bull listened. He was very foolish – very, very foolish. She wasn't going fast enough for him. She wasn't going fast enough, so what does he do? He tries to get inside her – he tries to shift shape with her. Silly puppy. Silly noodle. No one – not the great Kadellin, not Shabab-el-Din, not Solomon himself could have done that – not even tried it. Why? Because it's impossible! There's nothing to shift shape with! You can't get into – what's she called?"

"Ms Minn," Sparrow repeated, bewildered.

"Ms Minn!" Puckel broke out into a great roar of laughter and immediately was shaken by a fit of wheezing. "Ms Minn," he choked, "Ms Mi-hi-hi-hinn. Well, anyway," he went on, recovering himself at last, "he was thrown back, as you saw."

"Yes," Sparrow agreed, "he went right through the window and then dashed off up the road."

"I'll tell you what happened," Puckel interrupted, "you don't have to tell me. Off he went, up the road, off up into the mountains, with no other idea in his silly head than to get up – yes, yes – into the tunnel." He paused, then added solemnly, "And to what is in the tunnel. Yes, young Sparrow, Bull's one thought was to make contact with the dragon – because Bull thinks quicker than you, and knew at once that the dragon of the story must be in these mountains."

"I wanted to get to the tunnel too," said Sparrow, "as soon as I started thinking about Ms Minn's story."

"Of course you did," said Puckel. "The dragon was calling you."

"Calling me?"

"In his sleep," Puckel said impatiently. "Didn't she tell you about that? Or had you decided to doze off just then?"

"Oh yes – she did say something about someone thinking he was in the dragon's dream," Sparrow said, "– and I was just going to ask you —"

Puckel snorted. "That's one way of putting it. But who does the dreaming, that's what no one can answer: the dragon, or the person who thinks of the dragon's dream? You're lucky, young Sparrow, you had a narrow escape. It could have been you, not Bull. It comes of not knowing what you want."

"I don't understand," said Sparrow.

"The trouble with telling stories about the dragon," said Puckel carefully, "is that he calls out in his sleep – to those who can hear. You heard it, and Bull heard it. He's too greedy, Bull, and he heard it too soon: he has never met me, he has not been given a gift of his own, he had no protection, and now nothing turns out as it should."

"So how did he change into Gogs?" Sparrow asked.

"Gogs was there too," Puckel replied, "led by the birds. Gogs wouldn't hear the call of the dragon: he has too much sweetness in him. But he tried to stop Bull because he was anxious about him after what happened in the class-room. There was a scuffle, the birds twittered and confused things, they slipped to the edge of the cliff…"

"But then where's Gogs?" Sparrow asked anxiously.

"Safe enough, in his own body," Puckel told him. "But asleep. Bull has him. Gogs is Bull, and Bull can't leave his shape."

"Why not?" Sparrow said.

"He has lost the power," Puckel answered. "Bull's shape is no longer hidden: anyone can see it now – so it's no longer his own. We all need a home, to come from and go back to. A shape-changer's home is the body he has kept hidden. Without it, he would simply float away – that's why Bull is imprisoned in Gogs' body now for his own good."

"So what can we do?" Sparrow said in horror.

"Oh, we'll manage something," Puckel replied vaguely, staring off out of the triangular mouth of the cave. Gradually his expression became grimmer, and his deep-lined old face began to look sad and haggard. "He can't change," he said, "but he can be changed into."

"Who could change into him?" Sparrow gasped.

"Not could, but would," Puckel corrected. "Only one creature would."

"Not – not the dragon?" Sparrow exclaimed. "But how could – I mean – I thought the dragon was huge!"

"Only to look at," Puckel said. "Don't be fooled by appearances. Oh, he wouldn't have much use for Bull's mind or Gogs' shape, not for long. But there's one use he can make of them."

"To get out of the tunnel," Sparrow breathed.

"To get out of the tunnel," Puckel repeated solemnly. "Precisely that."

Sparrow gaped. "What can we do?" he said again.

"We wait," Puckel snapped. "When the business that is being attended to is finished, we can move. Now sit quiet – your tongue's like a bell-clapper."

Sparrow obeyed, but after being quiet for a minute, he remembered the milkstone and, opening his hand, dumbly held the shining thing out for Puckel to see.

Puckel looked at it. "The third stone?" he questioned.

Sparrow nodded.

"Then the time has come," Puckel said. "Now there's not long to wait."

Sparrow couldn't answer. He seemed to have forgotten how to speak. Strange things were going on, beyond even the strange things that were happening to him. Puckel obviously knew something about Ms Minn – and he apparently knew her silly rhyme about the stones. Or maybe it wasn't so silly after all... What did Ms Minn know? Who was she? Where had she gone? Who was her brother? For a moment the ridiculous thought crossed Sparrow's mind that *Puckel* must be her brother – at any rate he didn't know of anyone else who lived up in the mountains – but then he realized that if he were, she ought to be already here.

As these thoughts crossed his mind, Sparrow noticed a subtle, secret movement among the shadows on the floor. A silent thing glistened and slid over the stones of the cave. Presumably Puckel's stick, in its snake disguise, was entering the cave. Quietly, it glided over to the table leg, wrapped itself round it and climbed, coil upon coil. At last the head shot up over the edge of the table, and Puckel, absolutely still until that moment, grabbed it. A moment later he held the strange, twisted, polished stick in his hand.

"The time has come," he said again, "and we must go."

Flying with Puckel was unlike any other flying Sparrow had ever done before. It was more like flying in a whirlwind. Puckel held on to Sparrow by the neck, like a bird of prey, and his green cloak swelled and billowed all around them while the air bellowed in their ears. Their speed was incredible.

Within minutes they were rushing down towards the railway line. They landed, and gradually the turmoiled air grew quiet around them. Right in front of them was the dark archway of the tunnel.

Puckel paused, and seemed to be listening. You could see the railway line for a little way after it passed into total blackness.

Puckel shook his head. "This is not good," he remarked. "Come on." And he stepped along the sleepers into the tunnel.

Gradually the light faded, until all that was left of it was a pinhead far behind them – except that it didn't seem far because there was no feeling of distance in the stuffy darkness. Sparrow's skin crawled with the dankness and the closed-in feeling of the tunnel. Minutes before, they had been flying in the light, in the free air. Now he felt as if the whole weight of the mountain were on them, crushing them into the darkness. He clutched on to Puckel's cloak, tripping on the unseen sleepers of the railway track.

For minute after minute they crept forward, almost without a sound, except when Sparrow tripped or kicked a stone. Puckel never tripped.

After an age of darkness, the old man stopped so suddenly that Sparrow ran into him. Puckel ignored his mumbled apology. "Light," Sparrow heard him muttering, "now we need some light."

Sparrow agreed with him, but said nothing. If Puckel was able to make light, he was thinking, why hadn't he done it before?

But the light that Puckel made was no thin candle-flame, nor wavering torchlight, nor even a pale magical glow. It was a burst of flame, a great orange-red fireball that enveloped them in a burst of heat and singed their eyebrows. With a husky roar, the fireball flooded the tunnel around them with reddish light, and slowly began rolling down the line away from them, casting fierce lights and shadows as it went.

On and on it rolled, while Puckel and Sparrow watched silently until it dwindled to the size of a football far along the long straight tunnel. It was so far away that Sparrow could no longer see Puckel when the old man murmured, "No, not a trace, not a sign, not a scale on the wall."

"Has the dragon gone?" Sparrow asked, as relief flooded over him.

"Gone he has," Puckel confirmed.

"What about Bull?" Sparrow asked, as panic rose to take its place.

"Bull, Bull, Bull," Puckel muttered, "there's only one use for Bull, and that's in a field of cows. I don't have time for him. Come on!"

And with that he seized Sparrow by the neck again, and they flew back along the tunnel. If the air had rushed and roared when they were flying outside, inside the narrow tunnel it was deafening, and Sparrow felt his eardrums were going to burst.

They rocketed out of the tunnel-mouth back into the dazzling air, and up, up, up they soared – as high as the swiftly-moving clouds where the sunlight still basked golden, although the sun was setting on the earth below.

There they paused and hung, and Puckel searched the tumbled ground spread beneath them. Sparrow looked with him for a little, but could see nothing, and as Puckel went on and on searching the ground, patiently, bit by bit, he became restive. If Puckel could see things in the bowl, he thought, why couldn't he have found out from that where the dragon was?

The mountainous clouds billowed up and drifted past, golden and crimson. Sparrow could see far down through the valleys to the dead lake. The sun was low over the low black hills, which he could now see clearly at the lake's end, and the black water glinted with sombre gold. Up in the clouds again, something glinted between the great misty golden shapes, catching Sparrow's eye. Then the clouds shifted and covered it.

Sparrow frowned, searching over and under the massing billowy shapes. Then – there it was again! Something that glinted and flashed in the late sunlight, something that must be very large and very far away. Could it be the dragon?

Sparrow didn't want to disturb Puckel just yet, intent as the old man was on the ground below. So he kept his eyes fixed on the golden glinting thing as it disappeared and appeared again amongst the high clouds. Whatever it was, it was coming nearer.

It was still quite small when Sparrow realized at last that what he was looking at was no living thing. The shape of it was now distinct. Something thin, pointed, like a piece of stick with another piece of wood nailed across it, though shining and glinting as though it were made of metal.

At the Third Stone

Sparrow had thought about aeroplanes, argued about aeroplanes, dreamed about aeroplanes, but what he first felt, looking at a real aeroplane at last when he had been expecting the dragon, was that there was something slightly sad about it. It looked so fixed and helpless, a thing that couldn't help itself, that had been thrown into the air and left to float or fall as chance allowed.

"An aeroplane," he murmured. "There are aeroplanes, and I can see one. A tube with wings out to the sides that don't flap. It's an aeroplane."

"Eh? What's that?" Puckel broke off his searching and looked sharply at Sparrow.

Sparrow pointed. "Look," he said.

"Quick, come quickly, come quickly!" a voice called behind them. And there was Gogs flying towards them, white-faced, his red hair flying back in the wind of his speed.

THE TIME HAS COME

"Have you seen the dragon?" Sparrow called.

"Yes," Gogs called back frantically – or was it Bull? – "it's this way, come quickly!" He turned and swooped down, with Puckel and Sparrow hammering down the air behind him. Down they plunged, nine hundred, a thousand metres, while the mountain tops rushed up towards them – and into a mist. When they came clear of it again, there was no sign of Gogs, but still Puckel flew on. It was only then that Sparrow remembered that Gogs might not even be Bull, but – worse...

He twisted his head round to see where the aeroplane had got. There it was: larger now, much larger than Sparrow had at first realized – but then he saw something else behind, something hurtling upwards as fast as they were hurtling down, something with a strange twisted lizard-like shape and tattery wings and flames billowing around it...

Sparrow's first glimpse of the dragon

was nothing like his first glimpse of the aeroplane. There was nothing sad or hopeless about it. This was a living creature that knew exactly what it was doing; dangerous, fearsomely intent.

A glimpse was all he had before he found himself grabbing at Puckel's arm, pinching and scratching, screaming at him to stop and look.

It seemed an age before Puckel did, and by then they were skimming over the mountain tops. Sparrow pointed behind them, screaming into the roaring wind.

When at last Puckel saw, he let out a roar that fairly shook the mountains. Sparrow clapped his hands over his ears and shut his eyes, for Puckel began spinning round like a tornado. When he dared look again, they were shooting upwards, and the dragon was straight ahead of them. There was still no sign of Gogs.

Fast as the dragon was climbing, Puckel was climbing faster, heading off the great green and golden beast.

Was it possible, Sparrow thought, that *that* had been in Gogs' shape a minute before?

All of a sudden, the dragon became aware of them. Although it did not check its speed or its onward, upward rush, it turned its head, let out a bellow like a mad bull, and shot out tongues of bright red flame. It seemed still too far away to do any harm, but a second later Puckel and

107

Sparrow were enveloped in warmth, then heat – then a scorching furnace blast. Puckel slowed, but a moment later they were clear again, unharmed, and closing on the dragon. Sparrow saw now that it was huge, huger than any lizard could possibly be, knotted, spiked, taloned, green with golden scales and skinny golden wings, horribly ugly and yet, somehow, beautiful too.

Suddenly it disappeared, and immediately afterwards Puckel and Sparrow were lost in the midst of a thick grey mist. They had risen into the clouds, and all was cold, wet and silent.

Just as quickly, they shot out again, still climbing into the darkening blue air. Sparrow heard a whining roar that was not the wind, nor the beast-like roar of the dragon. An evil-smelling smoke hung around them which set him coughing. Then Sparrow saw it full-size: they had come up out of the cloud and crossed behind the path of the aeroplane, which was thundering away from them with what looked like four red eyes glaring back from under its wings. Where was the dragon? Puckel paused and turned in the air, looking wildly about.

With an explosion of flame and smoke, the dragon burst up out of the cloud like a fish leaping out of a pond.

The noise drowned out even the noise of the aeroplane. The dragon roared, and roared again; and mingling with the smoke left by the aeroplane, the dragon's flame went spinning and coiling. For a moment, Sparrow could not understand what was happening, for the dragon had shot its flame away from them, not at them.

But in that moment, Puckel let go of his neck. Sparrow let out a scream and fell like a stone.

"Fly, you bonehead!" Dimly Puckel's voice – or was it the stick's? – came down to him as he plunged into wet grey cloud again. "Help them as you can!"

At first it seemed to him that he had forgotten how to fly. But after a little, Sparrow realized that that was because the cloud was so thick that he couldn't see which way he was going. When at last he emerged into the clear air, he found he was flying after all – though slowly, so slowly, it seemed, after the terrifying rush of Puckel's flight.

Sparrow saw the mountains and the setting sun first. And then he heard the din of roaring ruin above him. He looked up, and all became plain.

First he saw the dragon, but it wasn't flying straight – it seemed to be twisting and turning, as a cat might do if you caught it by the tail and swung it. A second later Sparrow realized why. Puckel was clinging madly to its tail. He looked like a tiny black blob at the end of the colossal stretch of the magical beast, but it was

109

clear that what the old man had hinted about his fantastic strength had been no boast.

But some way off there was a roaring cloud of flame and smoke spinning down towards the mountain tops. It was all so clear now, horribly clear: the dragon had attacked the aeroplane and set fire to it. That was what Puckel had meant when he yelled to Sparrow to go down and help!

Sparrow left the scene of the dragon-fight and followed the flaming aeroplane – though what he could do he had no idea.

Sparrow did not know how aeroplanes behave when out of control. Otherwise he would have realized that someone in this one was still desperately trying to guide it and save the people inside. First one way, then the other, it tilted, slanting all the while towards one of the mountains that stood out flat as a table-top and pillowed in a deep covering of snow.

Very slowly, it seemed to Sparrow, the aeroplane hit the mountain top, its wing slicing into the snow and scattering a fine white shower of flakes. Very slowly, the dark body followed the wing, and then the flaming tail, sending a billowing mixture of black smoke and white mist boiling and coiling up together. Just before the smoke covered it completely, Sparrow saw it sliding to a halt at the very edge of the flat top. It had tipped slightly over when it finally stopped moving. Sparrow raced down towards it, still with no clear idea of what to do, except that he must help.

Now he was directly above the crashed thing, he circled, coming down more slowly as he tried to see what was happening. The tail was still in flames, and more fires seemed to have broken out along the body and on the wing that stuck up in the air like a fish's fin. But a door had opened in the top of the body, and in the dark entrance something was moving.

The door was in fact in the side of the aeroplane, but because it had crashed on to its side the door was facing upwards, a black mouth out of which a tiny figure struggled, crawled along the body a little, then slid over the side, plopped into the snow and disappeared. An instant later a second figure appeared, even tinier.

By this time, Sparrow had realized what he must do. The tube was full of people: perhaps it was full of smoke too. They would have to be helped out as quickly as possible. He dived towards the door in the plane's body, where the second figure seemed to be hesitating, as if afraid to jump over the side to the snow below. A third head was appearing out of the door. Without another thought, he had skimmed in, grabbed the figure teetering on the side of the plane, and flown on past.

111

He barely had time to register it was neither as big nor as heavy a person as he had expected when, with a deafening crash, a blow hit him in the back, and sent him staggering forwards through the air. Somehow he held on to his burden, though he lost considerable height before he recovered and could fly properly down to land on a rock well below the mountain top.

Sparrow had never seen an explosion before, and did not know what happens in explosions. What had hit him in the back was the blast from the exploding aeroplane, which scattered pieces of it all over the mountainside. A tower of black smoke, orange-lit from underneath, was rising up from the mountain top, while through the darkened air all around them tiny pieces of metal came whizzing and smoking down on to the stones. Sparrow watched, open-mouthed, almost unaware of the body he was half supporting in his arms, as the black smoke raged and gradually grew less dense.

At last he took some notice of his companion. It was a girl, apparently about his own age, with hair that was probably meant to be blonde, but just now was extremely dirty. The girl was in a dead faint.

Sparrow looked down at her, and couldn't quite decide what was wrong. She looked unharmed, so he left her lying in a heap and flew back up to the mountain top.

There he looked around in amazement. Everything had changed. There was hardly a sign of the aeroplane except a fiercely burning thing like a huge twisted skeleton. The heat was tremendous. The snow was grey and sunken and all covered with water. There was a horrible smell in the air that he had never smelled before, and mixed with it a smell like burning feathers. There was no sign of life. The explosion seemed to have destroyed everything. The only person left alive was the girl lying down on the mountainside.

When he was older, Sparrow thought a lot about that moment – had nightmares about it too: that moment when he knew that the people who had been in the aeroplane were simply not there any more. But at the time, he felt nothing at all. He left the mountain top and flew back to where the girl was.

When he landed, he saw that her eyes were open, and staring at him, but she didn't move. Sparrow stood and watched.

At last she made a sound. She was clearing her throat. Her lips worked silently. Then the voice came: "What's your name?"

"Sparrow," said Sparrow.

"Sparrow," the girl repeated. "Is that because you can fly?"

"I was always called Sparrow."

"Oh," the girl said, and closed her eyes again.

"What's your name?" Sparrow asked.

The girl opened her eyes again. They were grey-blue eyes, like mist that was about to clear and leave a blue sky.

"It's Kittel," she said.

"Skittle?" said Sparrow, wondering vaguely if she was called Skittle because she'd been knocked down.

The girl made a little grunt, which was actually a short, painful laugh. "No," she said, "my name is Kittel, K-I-T-T-E-L," she spelled out.

But that meant nothing to Sparrow, who had never done spelling. "Kay, Eye... What?" he repeated, bewildered.

"Kittel. I'm called Kittel, that's all," the girl moaned tiredly.

"I'd better take you back," Sparrow said. "You can't stay here: everyone else has gone."

"I know," Kittel murmured, "I was very lucky."

"Come on," Sparrow said, and Kittel let him lift her up, away from the wrecked aeroplane, across the mountain tops, and down to the forest on the lower slopes.

Sparrow had been going to take the girl to Puckel's cave, but he quickly saw that she would never be able to climb all the way up beside the little dark stream. She seemed very drowsy, and kept closing her eyes. What had Puckel expected him to do? There was nothing

114

for it, he decided: he would have to take her home.

He really wanted to go back up and find out what had happened between Puckel and the dragon. There was no sign of them in the sky and the air was quiet – no sound of roaring or thunder. But he couldn't leave Kittel lying in the forest: she needed help. Sparrow realized what it would mean if he took her home: he would have to tell Murie exactly how he had found her, and give away the secret of his flight. But he scarcely stopped to think about that. He flew again over the forest in the gathering twilight, past the Cliff of Murie's stone, and down the slopes towards the village. He flew over the clearing where he normally started and ended his flights. He flew on down to the round green hill where his home was, and landed in front of the house, while Cairo – as once before – reared and snorted and went thundering off to the far end of the paddock. He sat Kittel down on the bench outside the house and flung open the door.

Darkness was falling, and the soft yellow lamps on their wall brackets were alight inside. Murie was in the warm kitchen as Sparrow rushed in. She looked flustered and cross, and Sparrow hadn't had a chance to speak before she turned towards him from the stove, putting her hands angrily on her hips.

"Sparrow," she said accusingly, "what have

you done with my milkstones? Did you take them to school without asking?"

Sparrow stopped and gaped. "No, I haven't touched them."

"Well, someone has," Murie returned, "and I've been alone in the house all day. It's not fair, you know, giving me things and then —"

"Honestly, Murie," Sparrow protested, "I never touched them, I –" And suddenly Sparrow remembered the third milkstone. But where was it? He had had it in his hand; he had shown it to Puckel. And then what? The snake had come in after that and he didn't remember anything more about it. Had he dropped it in the excitement?

"I found another one," he muttered, peering into the pouch at his belt, "but it's gone too."

"What are you saying?" said Murie irritably. "And why are you so late back from school?"

"School?" Sparrow frowned.

"School," repeated Murie dryly. "Down in the village with a bell in a little tower…"

"Oh, school!" he remembered. "School's over again."

"Over!" Murie exclaimed. "But it's only just begun."

"Murie," said Sparrow, "there was an aeroplane crash."

"A what?" Murie said. "What are you talking about?"

"An aeroplane," Sparrow repeated. "Once Grandad said he went in one, when he was very young."

"That was a daft story he used to tell," Murie retorted. "It was just a joke. He never flew."

"There *are* aeroplanes, Murie," Sparrow said steadily. "I know because I've seen one."

"Fiddlesticks," Murie snorted. And then she seemed to notice Sparrow properly. "Goodness, look at you! What a mess you're in! You're black from head to toe. Oh, Sparrow, your clean clothes..."

Sparrow interrupted. "I know," he explained. "I'm black because the aeroplane crashed, and there was a huge bang, and fire, and a lot of smoke. But I've rescued someone."

"What?" said Murie blankly. She thought Sparrow had gone quite mad. "You've rescued someone. Who did you rescue?"

"A girl," Sparrow said simply. "She's called Kittel. She's here, outside. I saved her just before the bang came. It was on top of a mountain."

Of course it never even crossed Murie's mind that Sparrow could be telling the truth, but what worried her was that he seemed so serious about his story. Was he really going mad? She didn't know whether to laugh or shout at him.

"How could you possibly save a girl from a

117

mountain top?" was all she could manage to say.

Just then a soft voice spoke behind her. "Because Sparrow can fly," it said. Murie wheeled round to see Kittel standing in the kitchen doorway.

Murie found it all too much: there were simply too many things all at once. The loss of her precious milkstones; Sparrow's flying; Kittel; and, in due course, Kittel's description of the world she had come from.

"What do you mean, the television's *for* something?" Murie exclaimed in wonderment. "What? You see people on that screen? What size of people, for goodness' sake? You speak to a telephone? What a crazy idea. What do you say to it? Are they all mad where you come from, or what?"

And the more Kittel tried to explain, the more confused Murie got. And when Kittel tried to tell her about electricity, it was the last straw. Murie actually fetched a wet towel from the wash-house and wrapped it round her head. "I'm fevered," she muttered.

Sparrow wanted to know if Kittel often went round in an aeroplane. "This was just the second time," she said, "but it was the first time on my own. I'd been away on holiday to my uncle's." This was impossible for Sparrow. The only person he had ever known go away when there was a holiday was mad old Ms Minn. And how could Kittel have been on her own when he himself had seen that there were other people in the aeroplane?

"Our flight was very late," said Kittel, "because there were so many other planes waiting to land." And Sparrow had a picture – half nightmare, half miracle – of a sky dark with the great roaring things with their backward-glaring red eyes circling towers and spires of stone like ravens round a crag.

So much was new that it was a mercy Kittel needed to sleep a lot in the first two days after her arrival. Then Sparrow and Murie would sit together in the kitchen in stunned silence, trying to digest it all. For Murie it was just plain bizarre, but Sparrow had the added complication of Ms Minn's story to deal with. He knew of course that all the wonders of Kittel's world were the inventions of the dragon – the same dragon that he had just seen destroying the aeroplane. But Kittel, it seemed, had not heard of any dragon. It was people who had invented everything, she insisted, just clever people. Then he remembered about the people being mad, and he wondered if Kittel were mad, too, though she didn't appear to be.

When she was asleep, Sparrow would constantly creep into the room just to look at her. It seemed so strange to think that there was only a wall of mist between Kittel's place and the mountains, and yet here she was, so different she was like a creature that had come down from the stars.

By the second day, Sparrow felt he must go and find Puckel again. Of course he had to tell Murie all about what had happened, because she had wanted to know how he could fly. She seemed to believe him quite easily: perhaps because so many impossible things had happened already. But he said nothing about Gogs or Bull or the dragon. Eventually, telling Murie where he was going, he flew off up into the mountain; and she watched him go, shaking her head in disbelief.

He found the old man without difficulty, but there was little comfort to be had from him. It seemed the dragon was secure for the time being. "I've got him here somewhere," he said, and bent down and rummaged about in the drawer behind the chair. When he stood again, he had a bottle in his hand. It was an ordinary clear glass bottle with a cork in the top, and a heavy green seal keeping the cork in. Sparrow could hardly believe his eyes: inside the bottle was the dragon.

It looked extremely cross, and when Puckel lifted the bottle for Sparrow to see it, it spouted smoke and tiny red flames at them. The smoke drifted up and gathered in a black clot in the neck of the bottle. At the bottom was a little rough pyramid of rock.

"I shrank him," Puckel explained, "but a stupid mountain went and got in the way of the shrinking spell and I let it into the bottle too. I shall have to put it back when I let the dragon out, because you shouldn't steal mountains and that's a fact."

"Why are you going to let the dragon out?" Sparrow protested.

"I have to," answered Puckel. "I've only got him here for the time being. You can't really shrink dragons, and I only managed because he hadn't woken up properly from being in the tunnel. I pulled him out of the sky and banged his head against a mountain and that knocked him out for a moment or two, just long enough to shrink him. But that doesn't mean that everything's safe – oh dear me, no. The dragon may be little, but he's slowly boiling up. Feel the bottle."

Sparrow reached out his hand and touched the bottle. It felt hot. Not so hot that you couldn't touch it, but pretty hot all the same.

"It's getting hotter all the time," Puckel said, "and when it gets too hot – ping! The bottle will split apart, out will come the dragon and grow to his proper size again in no time at all."

"Why don't you put it back into the tunnel before it can get out of the bottle?" Sparrow asked.

"Bull is there," Puckel replied.

"We'll have to get him out," said Sparrow.

"Easy, isn't it?" the old man replied. "We'll just go into the tunnel, whistle, 'Come along now, Bull, it's time to go home,' and along he comes!"

"Well – not exactly," said Sparrow, "but something like that."

"Can't you get it into that rock-hard skull of yours," said Puckel severely, "that things are *not easy*? Bull is in hiding and he is waiting. He is hiding from the people of the village, because he knows they will think he is Gogs, and he thinks they will think he has killed Bull."

"But they'd know he wouldn't do a thing like that!" said Sparrow.

"They would know, but does he know they would know? There is something you did not understand. Bull can't see anything clearly any more. The dragon has been in his – or rather Gogs' – shape once already, and more than anything Bull wants that to happen again."

"Why on earth?" Sparrow gasped.

Puckel shook his head sadly. "Ah now, that is a great why indeed. Why does Bull want to do everything the wrong way? Why did he send you to get magic gifts for him that he had no right to? Why does he keep things to himself? He's scared of being small, I suppose. But now he's walked into just about the deepest trouble he could have. He'll end up less than small if he's not careful: he'll end up nothing at all. If Bull took your shape, to you it would be like falling asleep. You would remember nothing of what he had done while he was in your shape. It's different with the dragon: if *he* takes on your shape it doesn't feel like being asleep; you remember everything the dragon does – it can even seem as if you did it yourself. You feel very powerful. That's all happened to Bull. It wasn't for long – just enough for him to walk out of the tunnel and then distract our attention from that bit of flying ironmongery – but it was enough. For that little time he felt what it was like to be the most powerful creature on earth. He remembers and he liked the feeling. In the end the dragon will devour his mind."

"But why?" said Sparrow.

"Why what?" Puckel snapped.

"Why does it want to?" Sparrow said.

"I never said it wanted to," Puckel responded. "I said it will. It can't help it. That's what dragons do. Sensible people keep away from dragons. You can no more expect the dragon not to devour Bull's mind than you can expect water to flow uphill."

"Isn't there something you can do?" Sparrow pleaded.

"He must do it," Puckel said sharply. "He must decide, simply, 'No, I will not have anything more to do with the dragon.' Returning him to his own body, and helping him to make this simple decision, are the two things that must be done for Bull."

"And what about the dragon?"

"Eventually I will free him from the bottle. I will go into the tunnel and try to make sure that he is facing inwards and not outwards. But I cannot do this until we have got Bull and Gogs to safety. Nuisances they are – nothing but nuisances. I should never have listened to you. This has all happened because of you and your silly wishes. Now go away and leave me in peace. Come back in three days' time and I'll give you a rope and some other stuff."

And that, very suddenly, was the end of the conversation, for Puckel and the cave vanished and Sparrow was left, once again, floating in the air above the forest.

KITTEL

Sparrow drifted homewards. There was an unpleasant feeling, like a dark mist, hanging over everything: a feeling of threat, a feeling that things weren't running in their proper courses. He was also annoyed that he hadn't been given a chance to tell Puckel about Kittel.

When he got home, Sparrow found Murie had a visitor. It was Plato Smithers, the master-builder from the village. Smithers was also a kind of policeman in the village, and he had come to investigate the strange goings-on.

The village folk had no idea about Puckel or the dragon or about the magic powers Sparrow and Bull and Gogs had been given, or even about magic of any kind. But what they did know seemed strange enough.

This is how it looked to them: Ms Minn had opened her school again after one of her long absences. But on the same day that she opened it, she had started babbling some nonsense about a mad inventor of some kind, and in the middle of it had suddenly gone over to poor Bull, picked him up by the throat and thrown him right out of the school-room window. Just how that dry old stick had even managed to pick up a big strapping lad like Bull – let alone throw him through a window – was a complete mystery, but thirty-six children had seen her do it. Then she had stormed off without a word to anybody and had not been seen since. The fire in her little cottage on the edge of the village was out and had not been re-lit, and her cat was sitting on the doorstep looking very hungry and cold.

Everyone thought Ms Minn was a bit dottled anyway, but it was a lot more serious when they found that Gogs and Bull had disappeared as well.

On the day after Kittel had arrived, the men from the village went into the mountains to look for the missing boys. They found no sign of Gogs, but it was not long before they found Bull's body lying on the rocks under the cliff. It took them all day to get down there and attach ropes to pull it up.

When they took it home, Bull's grandmother got such a shock that she had to take to her bed. Gogs' mother was not much better – and of course she didn't even know whether her son was alive or dead.

However, a big argument now broke out over Bull. The old doctor from the village was brought to look at him, and he insisted that Bull was not dead at all. Nobody believed that you could fall off a cliff like that and survive, and as far as anyone else could tell Bull was dead as dead could be. They thought the old doctor had gone mad. But the doctor was very definite. Nor did he stop at insisting that Bull was alive: he also said that although many bones in the boy's body had been broken, they were already healing – in fact healing far more quickly than broken bones usually do. Bull narrowly escaped being buried, and was wrapped up warmly and laid in his own bed instead.

The day after Bull's body was found, Plato Smithers started his investigation. So when Sparrow came back home from seeing Puckel, he found Murie and Smithers sitting together in the kitchen with very serious expressions on their faces.

Had Sparrow known anything about Bull's death? they wanted to know. Sparrow said he hadn't. It was a lie, really, but Sparrow told himself it was pretty nearly true, because he didn't know anything about Bull's *death*: Puckel had said Bull was alive! What about Gogs? Smithers asked. Sparrow said he had last seen him heading towards the old railway tunnel. That was true enough. Had Sparrow been to the tunnel? Smithers wanted to know. Yes, said Sparrow, he'd been there to look for

Gogs, but hadn't found him. That was true, too.

Sparrow found to his dismay that Murie had told Smithers about Kittel. And then – to his relief – that she had not told him everything. She had been very sensible and simply told him that Sparrow had found her wandering about the mountains in a daze. Smithers went into the room where she was in bed. Thankfully she was asleep, or she might have told all. Smithers said he would send a message through the mountains to the next village to see if anyone had lost a small girl. Sparrow was quite surprised to hear Smithers saying this, because he had never heard anyone talk openly about the other villages before. Then Smithers left, shaking his head and saying it was all a terrible tragedy.

You don't know how bad it really is, thought Sparrow, as he watched the big man walking down the steep path from the house.

Kittel recovered so quickly that when Plato Smithers returned two days later, she was up and about. Sparrow and Murie had warned her not to say anything about where she really came from, and Kittel quite understood: in the city where she had lived the people were exactly like the village people and never wanted to speak about magic. She also saw that Plato Smithers would consider that an

128

aeroplane had quite as much to do with magic as any dragon.

Smithers said he had heard no word about a girl gone missing in the mountains and he wanted to speak to Kittel. But however many questions he asked her, Kittel just put her hand on her forehead and said, "I can't remember anything." She said it in such a high waily voice that Smithers was quite convinced that she really had lost her memory, though Sparrow and Murie had a hard job keeping straight faces. Smithers said Kittel might as well stay with them until they found out more about her.

This she was perfectly happy to do. She didn't behave like someone who had narrowly escaped from a plane in which everyone else had been killed. Sparrow found this odd but Murie explained that the shock of the crash had probably really made her forget things. Meanwhile Kittel was delighted with everything in Sparrow's house.

"I like the light of the lamps better than electric lights," she said, "and I'm sick of television and I didn't want to come back from holiday yet anyway." She was fascinated by the old crossbow in the hall, and she loved the cats and wild old Cairo out in the paddock, and the goats and the cow and the ducks with their waggling tails, and the lizard that scuttled across the kitchen floor every morning and every night. She had only a dog, she said, in her home in the great city where her mother and father lived.

"I'm going down to the village," Murie told Sparrow the next morning, "so you must look after Kittel. Don't let her go too far from the house."

But soon after she had gone, Sparrow, clasping Kittel, flew swiftly over the forests. As they flew a strange thing happened. Talking with Kittel, telling her all about the extraordinary happenings of the last three weeks, Sparrow suddenly found he could remember Puckel's name! This had never happened except when he was on his own or actually with the old man.

They landed at the foot of the little dark stream, but as soon as they had reached the high place where it rose in the courtyard of rocks, Sparrow saw that something was wrong. Mist was rising from the bubbling water. "It was never like this before," he muttered.

"Puckel!" he called softly. "Puckel, are you there?"

"Just here," said a quiet, watery sort of voice, out of nowhere in particular.

"Where are you?" Sparrow turned round, puzzled.

Suddenly Kittel laughed. "He's there, Sparrow, look: he's hiding in the water!"

"Where?" said Sparrow, even more bewildered. "I can't see anything."

"There!" Kittel sounded impatient, but she was still laughing, pointing down at the water as it bubbled and chuckled up out of the ground.

"He can't possibly be hiding there," Sparrow said, "he'd never fit in."

"I can see him though," Kittel insisted. "He's hiding there, he's looking up at us, he's – oh! he's disappeared."

"Did you say you could see me?" Puckel's voice suddenly came from behind them. They wheeled round, and there he was, leaning on his stick, as large as life, but with an expression on his face Sparrow had not seen before. For a moment he thought that the old man actually looked offended.

"Did you say you could see me?" he repeated, looking at Kittel.

Kittel wasn't laughing any more: she looked a little scared. She nodded.

"Come here," Puckel ordered.

Kittel went up to him, hesitantly. But when she stood in front of him, Puckel reached down and ran his brown hand through her golden hair, very gently, for a minute or two. "Hmmm," he said at length. "Hmmm, Hmmm. Well, that makes a big difference, now, doesn't it?"

"This is Kittel," said Sparrow. "I found her."

Puckel snorted. "She found you," he corrected. "These eyes saw through the dragon-mist, and not many could have done that. Could yours?"

Sparrow understood properly then that the mist that lay all around the mountains was the dragon's breath that made the mountains invisible to people from the world outside. He shook his head.

Puckel turned back to Kittel. "A gift as natural as daylight," he remarked, "and as rare as milkstones."

"I saw her though," Sparrow broke in, "and the other people on the plane."

Puckel screwed up his eyes. "The time and the place," he said mysteriously. "The dream of the dragon and the one who wakes in the dream of the dragon. This breaking through of a thing from outside has long been expected."

Sparrow felt less than satisfied with this, but there was something about Puckel's manner which suggested he wasn't prepared to say more on the matter. Instead Sparrow asked, "Why is there mist over the water?"

"Haven't you ever put your jug of milk in a stream to keep it cool?" Puckel demanded.

"Yes, of course," said Sparrow, "but —"

"Well, that's what I've done with my bottle of dragon – put it in the stream to keep it cool."

"It's like an electric kettle!" Kittel exclaimed.

"The dragon in the bottle's bringing the water to the boil!"

"It's no joke, by no means, not at all," Puckel broke in. "And I can assure you the water by itself isn't enough to keep him cool: I have to spend most of the day in the stream myself. It's very tiring, and it doesn't leave me any time for the other things I should be do-ing – like making it possible to get the dragon back into the tunnel."

"So you *were* hiding – no, you were shape-shifting," Sparrow exclaimed. "You'd turned into the water of the little dark stream! So how did Kittel see you?"

"You want to watch your step with golden-haired Kittel, young Sparrow," Puckel chuckled. "You won't keep many secrets from her, no indeed! You want to keep her as your friend, that's what you want to do."

"She is my friend," Sparrow declared.

"Good, good, good," said Puckel. "Then listen, for we haven't much time left. The dragon is growing hotter by the hour, and I will not be able to hold him for very much longer. Bull is in the tunnel, in the shape of Gogs. If this continues, Gogs will wake up a little inside his own body, and Bull will go to sleep a little, and you will be left with a dopey, half-witted sort of person inside Gogs' shape which is not Bull and not Gogs but a little bit of both of them. That is not good by any manner of means. And if Bull cannot be freed from the dragon's hold on his mind, then Gogs will be lost with him. So this is what must be done."

Puckel explained his plan, and though neither Sparrow nor Kittel liked it much, they agreed it was the only thing they could do and that they must set out right away to do it.

Soon they were ready to leave. Sparrow was carrying some things Puckel had given them which he said they would need. There was the rope he had promised – a silken-smooth thing, light as a feather, which Sparrow slung over his shoulder – a package of bread and cheese and two apples ("Not magic," Puckel said, "just plain, ordinary grub.") and a strange short, fat stick with a white ball on the end of it, rather like an overgrown clove in shape. Puckel described this to Kittel as "not merely a torch, but a multi-purpose implement." He was very precise in explaining exactly how everything was to be used.

"There's just one problem," said Sparrow.

"What's that?" Puckel snapped.

"I can't shape-shift," said Sparrow. For Puckel had suggested shape-shifting as a way of making his plan work.

But the old man looked very hard at Sparrow and said, "Yes, you can."

"Since when?" Sparrow said in confusion.

"Since Bull fell, of course," said Puckel.

"You felt the jolt, didn't you? That was the power passing into you."

Sparrow was staggered. He remembered the jolt well enough! And ever since then, if he had wanted to, if he had only known...

"What Bull had was yours by right," said Puckel sternly, "and to give it to you I have taken it back from where it should not have been given. When the rope is used, Bull will have the power to change shape once more, but only once: and he must be made to change back to his own body. If he does not, then the only thing that will save him will be the first light of the sun on the place that is not on the mountain and not in the valley, and finding that place is no easy matter. Now go!"

In a moment, with Kittel holding Sparrow tightly round the waist, they were in the air and high above Puckel's courtyard. They turned and sped down towards the distant tunnel.

They landed on the railway line. "How could you see Puckel when he was shape-changing?" Sparrow demanded.

"I don't know. I just could," Kittel shrugged.

"I'm going to turn into something," Sparrow said, "and I want to see if you can see me."

"Hurry then," said Kittel, looking anxiously towards the tunnel.

The real reason for Sparrow's suggestion was that he wanted to see if he really could shape-shift. Next moment he had slipped out of his own shape and into that of a nearby rock as easily as changing his clothes! It happened so naturally that the only way he knew that he had actually changed was because he suddenly found himself hard and cold, without movement or breath or any need to breathe, and he could see all round him at once, though to be sure everything, including Kittel, looked very dim and shadowy. He saw straight away what Bull had meant when he told Gogs that you couldn't see things properly. His strange rock-vision amused Sparrow immensely, but he could understand that Bull wouldn't have liked it much: you had to let go of yourself, somehow, to enjoy it, and Bull never did that.

"You're hiding in that rock," Kittel said, looking straight at him.

Sparrow was so surprised – at himself and at Kittel – that he changed back into himself again. "Have you always been able to do that?" he said.

"Do what?"

"See people when they've changed into another shape?"

"I never knew people could change into other shapes till you told me about Bull, so how could I?"

Sparrow opened his mouth to say something, forgot what, and closed it again. In fact he even forgot to be amazed at his wonderful new power because he was so amazed at Kittel.

But Kittel didn't seem to be amazed at anything. "Come on," she said, "we don't have much time."

They ran up the railway track and came to the mouth of the tunnel. There was no sign of anyone.

"Don't hide in anything too difficult," said Kittel, "or I might miss you."

"I just hope I don't get mixed up and turn into something I didn't mean to be," said Sparrow.

"Practise a bit when I'm in the tunnel," Kittel advised.

With that, she turned and went under the dark archway. Sparrow still had Puckel's rope, but Kittel took the bread and the cheese and the stick with the globe on it. As she disappeared into the darkness, Sparrow, watching from outside, saw the stick gradually begin to glow softly, casting a golden halo of light round Kittel. The light dwindled into the distance, but soon Sparrow heard Kittel faintly calling, "Gogs! Gogs! Are you there? Look, I've got food for you!"

Quickly, Sparrow looked about him. What was there? There was a thorn bush, a rock, a rowan tree still full of golden-brown leaves, a blackbird in the tree, the sleepers on the railway line, a rabbit peeping out of its burrow thinking Sparrow couldn't see it.

One by one, Sparrow quickly changed into all these things (except the rabbit) as quickly as a bird hopping from branch to branch. He went stiff and many-branched and prickly with the thorn bush, hard and cold and cracked with the rock, waved tall and gentle with the rowan tree, pirouetted and went "trr-tucka-tucka-tucka-tuck" with the blackbird, and lay flat on his back, heaving up at the steel line, with the railway sleeper. No wonder it's called a sleeper, Sparrow thought to himself as he changed back into his own shape: he had started to doze off!

He missed the rabbit because it had scuttled off when the blackbird sang. Sparrow wondered what he had said in the blackbird's voice that had so frightened it.

He wasn't sure what shape to take while he was waiting. The sleeper would have been a good choice if it had not made him feel so drowsy. He tried changing into the railway line itself, but that made his vision so thin and stretched-out that he was afraid he would not notice Kittel when she came out again. Then he saw the spider crawling up a mossy crack between two bricks on the tunnel arch. He changed into it, and began his wait.

He would have had a splendid view, because

he was right above the railway line – except that his spider's vision wasn't good enough to make things out at any distance. Then he remembered that he could spin a web, and softly let himself fall from the top of the arch. He felt the spider's cord unravelling itself swiftly from somewhere on his back, a pleasant, slightly tickly feeling. The cord felt amazingly strong and secure. Sparrow hung upside-down over the railway line in his spider's form and peered into the darkness of the tunnel.

Perhaps because a spider's brain is so slow (for some things anyway) he felt he had hardly waited any time before he saw Kittel's light approaching again. He tensed, straining his eyes to make out if she was alone.

No. There was someone with her – Gogs! It was Gogs walking beside her.

He looked so pale and thin! Sparrow hardly recognized him, though admittedly everything did look a little strange upside-down. With a shock that made him drop half a metre on his cord, Sparrow realized what it must have meant for Gogs to have gone without any food at all for nearly a whole week. What had Bull been doing? If he'd let Gogs' body starve to death, how could that have possibly helped him?

Sparrow suddenly felt very sorry for both Bull and Gogs. He had been so happy with his magical power, flying through the mountains, but Gogs and Bull had had nothing but trouble from theirs. It seemed unfair.

Now Kittel and Gogs were almost below him. Dimly, high in the distant air, his spider's eyes could make out a blur of shadow which Sparrow guessed was the rowan tree he had turned into before. He turned into it again. Kittel and Gogs were coming straight towards him – they seemed far below, because he was now four metres tall.

Kittel looked straight at him and grinned. "Come on," she said to Gogs, "we'll sit under the tree. I've got some bread and cheese for you now, and you'll feel much better after you've eaten it."

Gogs – or Bull rather, in Gogs' shape – was looking around warily. He was obviously afraid he might be walking into a trap. This was precisely why Puckel had said Kittel should go into the tunnel to fetch him out: because she was a total stranger, Bull wouldn't think that she had been sent by the village people. Now Kittel took his hand and led him over to the tree. If Gogs' body had not been so weak with hunger, Sparrow thought, Bull might have struggled – he might even have tried to take the food from Kittel by force. But he didn't. He let himself be led, sat down on a root of the rowan tree and waited for Kittel to unwrap the package of food.

Before Kittel did this, she put down the

torch she had been carrying. Bull-in-Gogs'-shape looked at it lying on the ground beside him.

"Where on earth did you get that?" he mumbled.

"I was given it," Kittel said. "I have some very strange friends."

Bull-in-Gogs'-shape frowned. Sparrow could see he was puzzled by Kittel.

"It looks magical," Bull remarked. "Are you a fairy?"

Kittel gave a very un-fairy-like guffaw. "There's no such thing," she scoffed. "There's no such thing as magic either."

"I wish you were right," said Bull.

BULL IN BONDS

Kittel unwrapped the bread and cheese, and handed it to Bull-in-Gogs'-shape. "Eat it slowly, and chew it properly," she ordered. "I've got another apple, if your mouth feels too dry." She put the second apple on the ground.

Then she sat beside him, first moving the torch back, so that when she sat it lay behind them. At the same moment she looked up into the branches of the rowan tree and nodded.

The blackbird was still sitting in the branches, eyeing Bull's bread with interest. Suddenly Sparrow took the bird's shape and fluttered down to the ground behind where Kittel and Bull were sitting. Bull jerked round at the noise, and almost choked; but when he saw it was only a bird, he relaxed again.

"You're all right," Kittel soothed. "No one's going to get you."

"How do you know so much about me?" said Bull-in-Gogs'-shape.

"I know lots of things," Kittel said teasingly.

"Can you understand the language of beasts and birds?" said Bull with his mouth full.

"Don't be silly," Kittel said, "people can't understand what animals and birds say."

"I can," said Bull.

The blackbird that was Sparrow hopped softly towards them. He put his three-toed foot on to the torch where Kittel had laid it in the grass. Then he took the foot off it and stretched a wing over it instead.

"Sometimes," Kittel said, "people who have a pet think they know what it's trying to say. But animals can't speak, not really."

"Well, I know what they're saying," Bull insisted. "I've only got to listen and I can hear them saying all kinds of things."

"What kind of things?" Kittel asked sweetly.

"Well," Bull began – he had finished his bread and cheese now, and was reaching for the apple. But he never got any further, either with the apple or with telling Kittel about the birds and beasts.

Soundlessly, the blackbird behind them had changed into Sparrow. For a split second he stood weighing Puckel's torch in his hand. The next instant he brought it smashing down on to Gogs' head.

There was a shattering sound like breaking glass, and a sweet drowsy perfume that for an instant floated past them. Bull-in-Gogs'-shape slumped forward, tipped off the tree-root and lay stretched on the ground.

Kittel leaped up. "Quick, the rope!" she cried.

Sparrow still had Puckel's rope slung round his body. Quickly now he unwound it. Although it was so soft and light it seemed very strong. A minute later, Gogs' body was bound round and round with the rope.

"Can you manage to carry both of us?" Kittel asked him anxiously as they prepared to fly off.

"I think so," Sparrow said. "Things don't seem to weigh very much when I fly."

They arranged that Kittel should hang on to Gogs, and Sparrow should hang on to Kittel. So first they had to heave Gogs' limp body on to its feet, and then Kittel got a good grip of him round the waist and held him upright. Then Sparrow took hold of Kittel's waist from behind, and leaped. "We're airborne!" Kittel shouted.

Bull had to be kept away from the dragon at all costs, so they couldn't go back to Puckel with him. Sparrow flew slowly down the mountain, over the forest, over the clearing, and straight home. They landed in front of the house, and laid Gogs' body down on the damp ground under the tall kale plants.

"Will that be all right?" Sparrow fussed.

Kittel was stretching and rubbing her aching arms. "Of course it will," she said. "Come on, let's get inside."

Murie was not yet back. That was good: it would look better if he was found by someone else.

All went according to plan. Half an hour later Murie came bursting into the house. "Gogs!" she cried breathlessly. "He's lying in the garden!"

"Gogs?" Sparrow and Kittel said together. Although he tried his best, Sparrow couldn't manage to act as surprised as Kittel. Her eyes went so round that for a second even Sparrow believed she knew nothing about Gogs.

"Didn't you see him?" Murie demanded. She was flapping about in the cupboard beside the fire, hauling out blankets and pillows.

Sparrow and Kittel shook their heads. "You told us to stay in the house," Sparrow said.

"I did not tell you to stay in the house," Murie retorted angrily. "I said you weren't to go far from the house. And he's lying out there in the blooming cabbage patch – you could have seen him from your bedroom window. He could have caught his death of cold. Come on, you'll have to give me a hand to get him in."

In a while Sparrow was running helter-skelter into the village. He had called at Gogs' house but there was no answer. So he ran straight down to Plato Smithers' house, where the big man was sitting in his office, still "conducting the investigation" with the aid of a bottle of parsnip wine.

An hour later about twenty people, Plato Smithers and Gogs' mother and father included, were crowded into the living room of Sparrow's house, gazing in disbelief at the still form of Gogs lying on the couch. He was still wound round with the rope from head to toe but no one so much as mentioned that. It did not take Sparrow and Kittel long to realize that, as Puckel had hinted, the rope was quite invisible to anyone else.

There was no argument over Gogs' body. Everyone agreed he was alive. He seemed deeply asleep, but no one was surprised at that, because they could see he was half starved.

He was taken on a stretcher over to his own house, and tucked up in his own bed with a roaring fire in the grate.

Sparrow and Kittel found him there when they walked over the next day. Gogs' mother looked at Kittel strangely, but she told them that Gogs had been awake for a while in the evening, although he was sleeping again now. They could go in and sit with him if they wanted.

Sparrow and Kittel went softly in. Gogs' head lay half turned on the pillow, his face pale and thin. He had his night-shirt on now, but even so they could still see Puckel's rope.

As soon as Gogs' mother had closed the door, Sparrow and Kittel bent over Gogs' body. Sparrow took him by the shoulder and shook him – though not too hard, in case the bed creaked.

"Come on, Gogs, please come on," he muttered, hopping impatiently from one foot to the other.

Gogs' eyelids flickered, but remained closed. "Come on, come on," Sparrrow said through his clenched teeth.

Kittel did not waste time hopping around. She pushed Sparrow out of the way, and bending over Gogs, gave him a vicious slap across the cheek.

"Kittel!" Sparrow remonstrated, but she ignored him. Gogs groaned, stirred, and a second later his eyes popped wide open.

His lips moved. "You said... You said..." were the only words that came out.

"I'm sorry," Kittel whispered. "I'm sorry I had to trick you."

"Bull," said Sparrow. "Bull, is that you?"

Gogs' eyes moved round and stared at Sparrow, cold and hopeless. Looking at his friend's eyes, Sparrow felt a knot in his throat as though he were going to start crying.

"Bull, please," he said. "P — I mean the old man – says you've got to change back into your own body right away. You and Gogs are both going to be lost and the dragon's going to burst out and everything'll be terrible. Please, will you change back into yourself and help us all?"

147

Gogs' face was still. Then it frowned. The eyes were hard.

"Will you do it, Bull?" Kittel said.

"My body's ... it's under the cliff," Bull said in Gogs' voice. "I can't go back to it. I'd be dead."

"It isn't," Sparrow told him. "It – you've been brought home. Your body's lying in your own bed. I – we – don't think you'll die if you change back into it. But think about Gogs. If you won't leave his body, it'll be like killing him, won't it?"

"Gogs tried to kill me," Bull said. "If I hadn't shifted into his shape, I'd be dead and he'd have killed me."

"He didn't try to kill you," Sparrow said. "It wasn't his fault; you've forgotten what happened. You just fell."

Tears sprang into Sparrow's eyes. "Please, Bull," he begged, "please do it. I – I just want my friends back, Bull and Gogs, the way they were before..." He had not meant to cry, but he felt he was losing the argument, and it was horrible how Bull seemed not to trust anyone.

"You've got *her*," Gogs' voice said, as his eyes moved round to Kittel. "You don't need your friends. You always thought you were better than us anyway – you went off and got magic powers without even telling us. That's just like you."

"That's not true," Sparrow sobbed. He sat

down and buried his face in his hands. Kittel
had turned away and was fumbling with
something at the bedroom window. Now she
came quickly back and slipped her arm round
Sparrow's shoulders.

The bedroom door opened. It was Gogs'
mother. She saw Sparrow sitting shaking with
sobs. "Come on, Sparrow," she said gently,
helping him up. "Gogs will be all right; you'd
better come out now."

"No!" Sparrow exclaimed. "You don't
understand – he's got to…"

But Kittel cut in, loudly and sternly. "Sparrow," she said, "Gogs' mum is quite right.
You're overwrought." And she gripped his
arm so tightly he almost yelled, and led him
out of the room.

When Sparrow and Kittel got outside they
walked silently away from Gogs' house and
started for home. Soon they passed the path
that led up to Bull's house. There was a tree
stump beside the road. Sparrow sat down on
it and groaned.

"What'll we do now?" he said. "Everything's spoiled. We won't be able to see Gogs
until tomorrow, and I'm sure we don't have
enough time. We'll just have to get Puckel,
that's all."

"No," said Kittel determinedly, "we can't
risk that. Puckel's busy keeping the dragon

cool, and if he's taken away, anything might happen. We've got to try everything we can."

"But what can we do? We can't make Bull leave Gogs' body and go back into his own. Only Puckel could do that."

"We don't know that even Puckel could," Kittel pointed out. "You mustn't give up so easily. Listen, here we are at Bull's house. That's where Bull's body is, right?"

"Right," said Sparrow.

"Then why don't we try taking Bull's body over to Gogs' house?"

"How?"

"You could change into Bull."

"But Puckel said no one's supposed to change into another person!" Sparrow protested.

"This is different," Kittel argued. "For one thing, it's an emergency. And for another, Bull's not really a person – I mean, his body isn't. It's just a body."

Sparrow had to see the logic of this, and somewhat unwillingly consented to try Kittel's plan. Quickly, they walked up to Bull's house. An old lady from the village was there to look after his sick grandmother and see if there was any change in Bull.

"Sparrow wants to see Bull, please," Kittel asked, very politely. And the old lady let them in.

A minute later, Bull was walking out of his bedroom with Kittel, towards the front door.

Of course Kittel knew that it was not Bull, only Sparrow-in-Bull's shape. But the old lady didn't know that. She fell down in a dead faint.

"Oh dear," Kittel said. But she kept going, and she and Sparrow-in-Bull's shape set off down the path again.

"Are you all right?" Kittel asked Sparrow.

"I – think so," Sparrow answered, "but I feel very strange. Bull's body doesn't feel right at all. I feel like I did when I was a tree."

"I think Bull's body must be a bit dead after all," Kittel said cheerfully. "You're a living corpse."

"Shut up," said Sparrow, "it's not funny."

Exactly what was wrong he could not tell. It didn't feel as though any bones were broken in Bull's body, and he felt no pain. But by the time they had reached the bottom of the path and started to walk on level ground, he knew he could not go on. He tried to sit down on the tree trunk again, but missed and crumpled on to the grass. "I'll have to change out for a bit," he mumbled, and did. Bull's body immediately tumbled over, the lids slowly closing on the bleared blue eyes. "Like one of those dolls with eyes that shut," Kittel murmured with interest.

"What'll we do?" Sparrow moaned. "I'll never make it at this rate."

Kittel was at a loss only for a moment. "I know!" she announced suddenly. "Let's get

151

Cairo!" Sparrow was about to object that Cairo would let no one near him, when Kittel added, "You can change into him and carry Bull and me."

Sparrow managed to move Bull's body out of sight behind the tree trunk. It lay looking pale and ghastly in the daylight.

They climbed up the white-pebbled path to Sparrow's house, and went straight round to where old Cairo's paddock was.

Cairo was standing in the corner of the paddock, looking very grumpy. He was holding one of his back hooves up off the ground as he always did when the ground was cold.

Sparrow got a severe shock when he shifted into Cairo's shape. Cairo, he suddenly understood from the inside, was old and cold and couldn't be bothered. He spent all his days longing for Sparrow's father to come home, and dreamed of eating sweet apples out of his master's hand. The horse's emotions were almost too much for Sparrow and nearly made him change back into his own shape again. But he held on, remembering the need for haste, and made Cairo's body run over the grass towards Kittel – strange and small and stick-like to his horse-vision. He relished the sound, *ba-da-doom, ba-da-doom,* of the heavy hooves pounding the turf.

Kittel used the gate to climb on to his back, and gripped him desperately with her knees as he picked his way down the steep path. When they reached the tree stump again, she dismounted and, going over to Bull's body, put her hands under his armpits and heaved him up. He was too heavy for her: she tripped over Bull's dragging feet, and both of them, girl and boy's body, jolted against Cairo's leg. Sparrow had to restrain his immediate reaction, which was to give Kittel a hefty kick. "You're so high!" she gasped. "I'll never get him on your back."

"What can I do?" Sparrow mumbled through his horsy teeth.

"You could lie down like a camel," Kittel suggested.

"But I'm not a camel," Sparrow mumbled. "I'm a horse." He didn't like the feeling that he was speaking through his nose.

"Don't be so stupid," Kittel snapped. "Look –" and she kicked him, hard, behind the nearer of his front knees. The knee buckled.

"Let your knees go, like that," she said.

Now Sparrow realized what she meant, and he let his knees go. Somehow his back legs followed, and soon he was lying on his stomach beside Kittel.

Kittel heaved and humped, and in a couple of minutes she had Bull's body sitting on Cairo's back, while she sat behind, holding him upright.

"Right, get up now," she ordered.

* * *

Bull-in-Gogs'-shape was lying awake in Gogs' bed. There was no one in the room with him – which was just as well because Sparrow didn't wait for Kittel to check. Gogs' bedroom window suddenly flew open, and Cairo's nose was shoved in.

Kittel had hatched her plan while they had still been at Gogs' house before, and quietly taken the catch off Gogs' window. Now she pushed Cairo's head out of the way, and peered down from his back into the room. "Hello, Bull," she said. "It's us again – we've brought your body."

Gogs' eyes stared at them, but Bull could not move because of Puckel's invisible rope.

"I don't want it," Gogs' voice muttered hoarsely.

Kittel ignored him. "Are you ready, Sparrow?" she said to the horse's ears. The horse's ears twitched back. "One – two – three – now!" And Kittel let go of Bull's body and swung her leg off Cairo's broad back. At the same moment, Bull's body came to life, because Sparrow had shifted into it. But as soon as Cairo became Cairo again, he reared and bucked and bolted, and Kittel and Sparrow were shaken from his back like turnips off a cart.

Kittel and Sparrow-in-Bull's-shape landed in a heap. "Are you all right?" Kittel said, and Bull's head nodded.

Bull in Bonds

Bull, looking through Gogs' eyes, could only gape in utter amazement as first Kittel, and then his own – Bull's – body clambered in through his – Gogs' – bedroom window and stood beside Gogs' bed.

PANIC

The shadows were gathering in Gogs' room. The short winter day was passing, and night was coming on fast.

Kittel whispered, not wanting Gogs' mother to know they had come back, "Bull, you mustn't be afraid. We want to help you." She pointed to Sparrow-in-Bull's-shape. "This isn't you, it's really Sparrow. And if Sparrow can go about in your shape, so can you, can't you?"

There was a long silence. At last Gogs' mouth moved, and Gogs' voice spoke. It was really Bull speaking to Sparrow, but it was Gogs' voice which spoke the words, and Bull's ears which heard them. "What does it feel like?" he asked.

Sparrow answered in Bull's voice, "It feels fine." It was not really true, because Sparrow felt so very strange in Bull's body – cold and sluggish and far-away – but he thought he had better not tell Bull that. "It feels just like me," he said, "only not quite like me, because it's a bit bigger – I mean, you're a bit bigger than me, if you see what I mean."

After another long silence Bull said, in Gogs' voice, "I don't think I can change. I tried to change before, when I was in the tunnel, and I couldn't. Nothing happened. And Gogs would wake up sometimes, and –" he stammered, and a catch came into his voice, as though he were trying not to cry – "I felt he was trying to eat me up. He would fight with me, and I'd rush about hitting myself, punching myself all over, and twisting my arm up my own back – well, Gogs' back I mean. It's not really my own back at all, I suppose."

"It must have been very nasty," Kittel said sympathetically. "But P — I mean..." She paused. "What's the old man's name, Sparrow? I've forgotten."

"So have I," said Sparrow. "I always do."

"Did you know his name?" Bull asked Kittel.

"Yes," Kittel said, puzzled.

"I never knew it," said Bull. "I don't think he could have liked me."

As Bull spoke, Sparrow realized his friend had changed. To begin with, he had thought it might just have been because it was Gogs' voice he could hear and Gogs' expressions – or nearly Gogs' – that he could see, and of course Gogs was always trying to patch up the quarrels that threatened to break out between Bull and Sparrow. But as Bull spoke, he saw that it wasn't just this. Bull, he understood, must have been through a terrible time. He had very nearly died, he had lost his own body, he had been starved, he was frightened, and inside him there was someone else – his own best friend – who he knew might wake up at any time and try to destroy him. Dimly it came to Sparrow that, whatever happened now, Bull could never be the same again – never again be that secretive know-all who was their leader and who took all the decisions. And, now that he knew this, it made him feel sad – sad that their friendship had changed, and sorry that it had changed because of him.

"Well, anyway," Kittel told Bull, "the old man wants to help you. You see the rope you've got around you?"

"It's a magic rope, isn't it?" said Bull. "No one else could see it."

"Yes, it is," Kittel agreed.

"I thought you said there was no such thing as magic," Bull said.

"I was tricking you," Kittel replied. "I'm sorry. But it was just because we all wanted to help you. P — the old —"

"We call him Piddle," Bull put in.

Kittel looked doubtful. "Anyway," she went on, "he says that if we take the rope off you, you'll be able to shift your shape one more time."

"And never again?" Bull said.

"I don't know about never again," Sparrow said. "I'm sure if you went up to see him and asked him properly, he'd let you do it again." Though he was not sure at all.

"Are you a shape-shifter now?" Bull asked wistfully.

"Yes," said Sparrow, "I became one when you fell. Look."

He sat down against the wall. And then quickly, effortlessly, as if he were pulling off his clothes, he slipped out of Bull's body, and stood there, Sparrow, in his own proper shape. "See?"

"If I can only shift shape once more," said Bull, "do you mean I have to go back inside that?" – and he nodded towards his body, slumped against the wall like a rag doll someone had thrown away.

"You'll be all right," Sparrow assured him.

"I want to see you shape-shifting," Bull announced suddenly.

"Why?" Sparrow asked.

"Go on, just do it – change into something else."

"All right," said Sparrow. There was a bowl of Christmas roses by Gogs' bed. Sparrow changed into one of them. "Hello, here I am," he said in the flower's voice.

Bull grinned. It looked just like Gogs' normal wide silly grin. It was hard to believe

159

that it was Bull grinning and not Gogs. "I like that," he said. "Now be yourself again."

Sparrow changed back into himself.

"I want you to change into that horse again," Bull demanded.

"Cairo?" Sparrow said. "He ran away. There's no sign of him."

"He's not far," Bull said. "He's eating the raspberry canes in the garden."

"How do you know?" Sparrow said.

"I heard him just now," Bull explained. "He said, 'This is the best thing I've tasted for years. I'm not going back to eating that muck in the paddock again.'"

Sparrow had forgotten Bull could still understand the language of beasts – or was Bull using Gogs' power? "I'll change into Cairo if you really want me to," he said, "though I don't really see why you do."

"Please," said Bull.

Sparrow clambered out of the window and disappeared into the deepening twilight to look for the horse.

"Will you take off the rope now?" Bull said to Kittel. "I'll change back into me while Sparrow's out, I don't want him to see me do it."

She pulled back the bedclothes, and untied Puckel's rope from Gogs' ankles, pulling it through from underneath him, unwrapping him bit by bit. She unwound it from his neck,

160

and so came to the last knot. "All right?" she asked encouragingly.

"All right," Gogs' head nodded.

Kittel untied the last knot. Stiffly, Bull-in-Gogs'-shape got up. He crossed the floor to where his own body was sitting propped against the wall, and knelt down beside it.

At that very moment, Cairo's head pushed through the window again. "Hello," he snorted, his mouth full of chewed-up raspberry leaves.

Kittel sighed. "Just go away a minute, Sparrow," she said.

"No, it's all right now," Bull said, looking up at Cairo's head. "I don't mind now. I'm ready. You come in, Sparrow," he said. "I want you here with us."

What followed took less than ten seconds, though it takes longer to describe it.

First Sparrow changed out of Cairo's shape. Kittel saw him climbing in through the window, beside the horse's head. Cairo's eyes looked utterly confused for a moment, and he stopped chewing his raspberry leaves. Then he noticed Sparrow climbing past him, and lunged his mouth round to give Sparrow a vicious nip on the bottom.

Sparrow yelled and fell forwards, tripping over Bull's legs on the floor and knocking over Bull-in-Gogs'-shape as he was kneeling beside his own body.

161

"Ow!" Gogs' voice exclaimed, as Sparrow fell on top of him. But immediately afterwards Sparrow felt Gogs' body go quite limp, as if it had suddenly fallen asleep.

Meanwhile Cairo swung his head round, smashing the glass in the window, and then – "Quick, Sparrow!" Kittel yelled at the top of her voice. "Turn back into Cairo! Quick! Be quick!"

Cairo was looking dazed, and beads of blood were breaking out beside his nose where the glass had cut it.

Kittel screamed again, "Sparrow! Sparrow!" But Sparrow was dazed too, kneeling over Gogs' body lying on the floor. What brought him to his senses was Kittel's savage kick in his ribs. "Get off your knees, you idiot, and get inside that horse!"

Sparrow looked round to the window. Cairo was just rearing up, tossing his mane. Without another thought he changed, and even as he took on the horse's shape, panic seized him and he was carried away on the horse's hooves in a frenzied gallop.

At that moment, in the house behind him, the bedroom door flew open and Gogs' mother and father rushed in. They saw the smashed bedroom window hanging open and Gogs lying on the floor with Bull's lifeless body slumped beside him, and the girl Kittel standing in the middle of the floor, screaming wildly.

162

Gogs' mother started screaming along with Kittel, and Kittel saw that the best thing she herself could do was to carry on.

So it was left to Gogs' father to pick Gogs up off the floor and carry him back to his bed. For a moment, Gogs' eyes opened. "Oh, I'm glad to see you again, Dad," he muttered, and then went back to sleep.

Meanwhile, Sparrow-in-Cairo's-shape was galloping through the gathering night uphill over a field of rough grass. He had forgotten he was Sparrow, forgotten about Bull: he was almost all horse.

What saved him was the fence. It loomed up right in his path, and the horse swerved from his headlong gallop. Cairo had grown fat from not working, and could not have jumped. He ran along beside the fence, snorting, shaking his mane. Soon the land was sloping downhill again, and he galloped faster.

The fence flicked by, post by post. As this was the field Kittel and Sparrow had come through to get to Gogs' bedroom window, the gate was still open, but the horse was running the wrong way to come to it quickly: before Cairo could find the gate he would have to pass the house again.

And it was the screaming from the house which cut through the rushing of the horse's panic. Cairo's ears heard the screams, and he reared up, fell on to four feet again, then stood stock-still, listening.

It was just what Sparrow needed. He remembered straight away that he was Sparrow and not a horse, and when he heard the screaming he thought he had better become himself again. He would have changed back into his own shape then and there but just in time he remembered about Kittel's having been so anxious for him to change into the horse. And as he thought about this, he realized that being Cairo did not feel at all the same as it had done before. There was a breathless, confused feeling about it, almost as though he were being squashed.

Cautiously, he edged forwards to the open window of Gogs' bedroom, where a light was now shining.

At first it was difficult to make out what was going on inside the room: he was looking through a horse's eyes, and horses' eyes are made for being outside and looking at the weather and grass and gates, not for peering into bedrooms.

Gradually he made out the bed, and Gogs lying in it, asleep. And Kittel standing beside it, and – Bull still sitting slumped by the wall. What was wrong? Sparrow wondered. Why hadn't Bull got up?

Gogs' mother was nowhere to be seen, but just then Gogs' father came in. Kittel had apparently just finished screaming, and Gogs' father patted her on the head, then bent down and picked up Bull and turned to carry him out of the bedroom. Kittel immediately looked up and saw Cairo standing outside the window. She frowned in a puzzled way. Sparrow-in-Cairo's shape moved closer to the window.

Suddenly Kittel clapped her hands against her cheeks. "Oh good gracious," she exclaimed. Then, "Wait outside the house, Sparrow," she ordered. "I'll be out in a moment. Don't change out of Cairo!" Then she turned and ran out through the door.

It was only a minute later that she had rejoined Sparrow in front of the house. "Come on," she said, "straight home. It is you, Sparrow, isn't it?"

"Yes, it is. What's wrong?" Sparrow mumbled. He couldn't get used to talking through a horse's mouth.

"I'll tell you when we get home. Can you come over to the fence so I can get up?"

Sparrow stood by the fence while Kittel scrambled up on to his back. Neither of them spoke until they were home again.

"Into the paddock," Kittel said curtly. "I think that'll be safe enough."

Sparrow-in-Cairo's-shape stood by the paddock gate until Kittel had tied it shut. "Now be Sparrow again," Kittel said.

Sparrow stood beside Kittel. Cairo stood

165

beside the gate, looking sorrowfully over at them. Kittel stared intently at him.

"Bull," she said solemnly, looking at Cairo, "that was a very silly thing to do."

Cairo turned his back on them and flicked his tail.

"What do you mean?" said Sparrow. "Why did you call him Bull?"

"Because it is Bull," Kittel answered. "Bull changed into Cairo instead of himself."

"But he could only change once more!" Sparrow exclaimed.

Kittel lowered her voice, so that Bull couldn't hear. "I know," she replied, "but after all, we did trick him before. Maybe he was so scared of going back into his own body that he thought he'd risk being a horse."

"Maybe he wanted to gallop off to the dragon," suggested Sparrow.

"Well, he didn't make it," said Kittel grimly. "And now he's a horse and he'll have to be a horse for the rest of his life."

"That won't be very long now," Sparrow whispered. "Cairo's an old horse – he's much older than me."

"I thought if you turned into Cairo straight away you'd push Bull out and he'd have to go into his own shape," said Kittel. "But it wasn't as simple as that. You were both inside Cairo's shape together."

"I hope that doesn't mean that I became Bull," said Sparrow anxiously, "because Puck —"

"I wish you'd stop rabbiting on about that," Kittel snapped. "Can't you understand everything's different in an emergency? Anyway, you didn't become him. You squashed him."

"Did I? I thought it felt funny, being Cairo," said Sparrow, "but I didn't feel Bull there at all."

"I don't think he's such a strong shapeshifter as you," Kittel said. "I could see you both inside Cairo, but Bull did look sort of squashed-up."

"What'll we do now?"

"Well," said Kittel thoughtfully, "I think you'll have to take Bull's shape again, and then try to get him over here. Of course! Once you've got him out of the house, you could fly and carry him! Why didn't we think of that before?"

"I've never flown round here, that's why," said Sparrow, scratching his head. "But why do you want him over here anyway?"

"We'll have to persuade Bull – Bull the horse, I mean – to carry us up to Puckel's cave so we can get Bull and Cairo sorted out. Remember Puckel said there was only one other way – something about being in the place that wasn't on the mountain or in the valley."

"In the first light of the sun," Sparrow

remembered. "But he said it wouldn't be easy."

"We'll have to take Bull to him all the same," Kittel answered. "He's the only one who'll know how to do it."

Sparrow looked doubtful. "All right," he agreed at length, "I'll go."

"Bull will be safe enough here," said Kittel. "He won't get out, and I'll try to talk to him. Bull's body is in a bedroom upstairs in Gogs' house, so you'll have to be careful no one sees you getting in or out."

"I'll be careful," Sparrow said. "I'll be straight back."

He flew off. Kittel immediately turned and started speaking softly to Bull. Although he went on flicking Cairo's tail at her at first, slowly he began to listen as she explained that he would have to see Puckel or he would stay a horse forever.

But Sparrow was back even quicker than he had said, and he was alone. Although it was almost completely dark now, there was enough light from the house for Kittel to see that he was looking very worried.

"Over here," said Sparrow, and led her to the side of the house where they couldn't be heard. "Bull's body won't move," he told her.

"What do you mean?" Kittel frowned.

"I changed into his shape," Sparrow said, "but I just lay there. I couldn't move as long as

168

I was in it. I felt like I did when I turned into the rock."

"You'll have to get Puckel down here now," Kittel said.

"I'll have to get Puckel down here now," Sparrow said at exactly the same moment.

When Sparrow had left Kittel and flown over to Gogs' house, it was almost dark. When he set off to find Puckel, the night came on in earnest. The sky was overcast with cloud, and it soon became too dark to see anything.

Sparrow was making his first flight by night, and within a quarter of an hour he was completely lost. But when he landed – quite by accident – on a rocky ledge somewhere close to the tops of the forest trees, he found that something extraordinary had happened. Standing on the ledge in the pitch darkness, he whimpered Puckel's name out loud, and to his surprise was answered by an owl, which whooed and wheezed once or twice before Sparrow understood it was saying it thought everyone knew where Puckel was. The owl turned out to have a very low opinion of Sparrow, but Sparrow was so delighted to discover that he had received the gift of understanding birds and beasts that he scarcely noticed its ill humour. He guessed this new power must, somehow, have come to him when Bull left Gogs' shape – though whether he had received

Bull's gift or Gogs', he could not know.

After being rather rude to him, the owl offered to guide him to Puckel's cave. Sparrow gratefully accepted, and the creature was luckily as good as its word: after a mere five minutes' flight it hooted that it was time to come down. Sparrow made a blind landing in the darkness, and as his feet touched the ground he tripped, took a big step, and landed, *splash*, in water. He let out a yell and jumped back. The water was boiling hot. Above him, he heard an owlish mutter concerning the stupidity of humans and sparrows, as the bird whirred off into the night.

Sparrow understood straight away that he was in Puckel's courtyard, but didn't stop to wonder that he had reached it by flying. "Puckel?" he called. "Are you there?"

There was no sound, except the bubbling and hissing of the little dark stream, hot against the cold rocks.

"Puckel?" Sparrow inquired again.

Still there was no answer. Sparrow did not wait longer. He took a deep breath, and changed.

Immediately, he felt as if everything were pouring out of him. On and on it went, as if it had never started and would never stop, pouring on, stretching out, pouring until he could not understand how there was anything of him left to pour. But there always was: more and more, oceans and oceans – any amount of water could go on flowing through him for hundreds of years.

He had changed himself into the little dark stream. But he scarcely had time to think what it felt like just then, for in a moment he was aware that Puckel was flowing beside him. Sparrow could see no sign of him, but he sensed that the old man was huffing and puffing there, very hot and bothered.

"Did you get him?" Puckel's voice murmured.

"Yes," Sparrow answered, in the murmuring voice of water. "At least, he made his last change. But everything's gone wrong."

"Wrong?" Puckel bubbled. "How, wrong?"

"He's changed into a horse," Sparrow answered.

"All is not lost," Puckel rippled. "When the first light of the sun falls —"

"I know," Sparrow interrupted in his watery voice, "but Bull's own body feels all wrong, and I couldn't move in it: I think it's dying."

"What?" A great spout of water burst out of the stream and broke into a cloud of steam.

"I'm sorry," Sparrow murmured. "We did the best we could. Isn't there anything you can do?"

Silence followed, a long liquid silence, in which Sparrow could feel eddies of icy, then boiling water, curling and slipping around him as Puckel thought.

At last, sadly but with resolve, Puckel answered. "You stay here," his voice swirled thickly, "and try to keep the dragon cool. But you must promise me one thing. You must promise me that if the dragon escapes, you will not change from the stream until he's gone – you'll let him go."

"But," Sparrow faltered, "he might attack the village!"

"You'll not stop him," Puckel's voice swirled again. "Now promise me, or else I'll not go to help Bull."

"All right, I promise," Sparrow told him.

"Think cool," Puckel's voice came. "Don't let the dragon trick you into feeling too hot." And Sparrow was alone.

The moment Puckel had gone, Sparrow felt himself bubbling like water in a kettle. The dragon was making him boil. What could anyone do against heat like that?

But gradually, despite the bubbling, Sparrow realized that the stream he had turned into was much more than just the water swirling round the bottle with the dragon in it. It stretched. It rose to the surface of the ground out of the depths of the earth, endlessly deep and endlessly cool.

He saw what Puckel had wanted him to do. He thought cool. He brought up more and

more coolness from the deep, sunless rocks
inside the earth, and wrapped it round and
round the bottle where the angry dragon
glared through the thick glass with its tiny, terrible, raging orange eyes.

Hours went by, slow watery hours with no
sense of time.

Sparrow stuck to his task, and as he grew
more used to the feel of the stream, his confi-
dence grew and he seemed to manage better
and better. In due course he began to feel
pretty pleased with himself. But even Puckel
had said it was tiring trying to keep the dragon
cool, and Puckel was much older and stronger
than Sparrow. After a while – it was hard to
say how long, but the night continued pitch-
black as ever – Sparrow wondered whether he
could keep thinking cool when all the time he
could feel the dragon thinking hot – oven-hot,
furnace-hot, volcano-hot. And as he grew
tired, he began to feel, quite unreasonably,
that Puckel had simply nipped off and left him
with the most dangerous and difficult task of
all. It wasn't fair!

Puckel should never have left him in charge
of a dragon which had once terrorized the
whole world!

Just as dawn was making the sky pale
Sparrow knew he had lost the fight. Try as he
might, he could not think cool at all. And now

the dragon had grown so big it filled all the bottle, coiled round and round and in and out of itself, its sides pressed against the sides of smooth glass.

And suddenly – *plick!* A crack was running through the glass of the bottle, all down its length.

Sparrow wasn't going to lie there and let the dragon get away with this! Without a moment's thought he changed himself into the bottle. He had some idea that as long as he could hold himself together, the dragon wouldn't escape.

But he had not reckoned on the heat and the pain. In the shape of the bottle, Sparrow felt as though his very bones were melting from the fire inside him. And the split that ran from his neck to his foot was like a red-hot whiplash. And then another crack ran through him. Another crack of the whip. And then another, and another, until Sparrow felt his bottle-body laced with cracks, up, down, from side to side, and all around him.

He yelled, and as if in answer, the dragon inside him roared. Very softly, but menacing, that roar began; then it grew, like an express train coming out of a tunnel, until Sparrow's whole brain was full of the roaring and he felt his head was going to burst.

Just in the nick of time, he changed back into the shape of the little dark stream, just as the bottle burst and its fragments spun off through the water. The water boiled, turned into steam, and dragon smoke gathered and rose up into the air.

Exhausted, Sparrow sank back into the water that was himself, and the little dark stream flowed on as he slept, unaware of the dragon which sat in Puckel's mountain court-yard, spouting black smoke and growing, growing, by the minute.

A JOB FOR KITTEL

"I don't mind being a horse," Bull said. "Being a horse is better than being dead."

"But you wouldn't be dead," Kittel said – though even she was no longer sure about this. She didn't try too hard to persuade him.

She tried another approach. "I like horses," she told the horse that had been Cairo. "At home I always used to go riding at the weekends. I've never ridden bare-back though."

"I don't like horses," Bull snorted. "My dad was killed by a horse."

"I'm sorry," Kittel said humbly. "All the same you'd better start trying to like them a bit if you're going to be one. And you must admit, you'll be an extremely clever horse – and you'll be able to talk."

Bull-in-Cairo's-shape seemed to think about this.

"Would you let me ride you?" Kittel asked after a moment.

The horse flapped his ears. "Perhaps," he huffled.

At that moment, with a thundering of the air and a small hurricane that sent Bull-in-Cairo's-shape bolting off into the darkness of the other side of the field, Puckel flew down out of the night and landed beside Kittel.

"Where?" he said, in a deep, commanding voice.

"Over at Gogs' house," Kittel replied.

"Show me!" cried Puckel, and seized Kittel by the arm as the hurricane whirled them off the ground again.

Puckel burst into Gogs' house just as the doctor was coming out of Gogs' room. The doctor had been pleased to hear that Bull had walked over to Gogs' house, because that proved he had been right about Bull not being dead. But when he went to the upstairs room where Bull's body had been laid, he took one look at him and said, "Well, he may not have been dead before, but he's dead now, in my opinion." Then he had gone downstairs to see Gogs, found him asleep, but quite healthy, and had come out to see if he would be offered any parsnip wine. That was when Puckel and Kittel entered the hall of the house.

"Where is Bull?" Puckel demanded in a voice that rattled the slates on the roof.

"And who might you be?" enquired the doctor, sticking his thumbs in his braces and peering at the wild-haired, wrinkled, green-eyed old creature in the moss-green cloak.

"I," said Puckel – and his voice, though quiet now, made the doors clatter in their frames and blew the dust from under the carpet – "am the boy's godfather."

"Never seen you before in my life," the doctor answered, "and let me tell you I know everyone in this district. Let me also tell you that young Bull is – regretfully – dead. If you're a relative, you may go up and see him. Otherwise, I think you had better go back to where you came from."

"Bull," said Puckel simply, on a soft high note like a bell. In a twinkling, the hall had transformed itself into the upstairs room, and Puckel and Kittel were standing beside the bed where Bull's body was laid, while downstairs the doctor was looking around in bewilderment.

Puckel got to work. First he sealed the door by drawing all round it with his thumb, muttering meanwhile. "Now no one can get in," he announced. Then he sealed the window in the same way – "And nothing can get out," he said. He put out the lamp beside the bed, but after a moment of darkness, the whole room began to glow with a deep yellow light, like golden moonshine. Then the old man propped up his stick in a corner of the room, went over to the bed and sat on it. He looked at the still body, utterly without movement under the bedcover, for a long time. Then at last, he took Bull's pale head in his lap. And slowly, softly, Puckel began to sing.

No one but Kittel ever heard that song, and what was in it she never told anyone, not even Sparrow. Quite possibly she could not have said, even if she had wanted to, because more than likely it was in no language that she could understand. But that song was something she never forgot, and for the rest of her life, if she stopped still and listened in a silent moment, she would hear it softly streaming from the wrinkled brown lips of the wild old man of the mountains.

It was a song of waking, a song of life, a song which would not leave sleeping things alone to sleep but made them move, breathe deeply, raise their heads, grow, stretch towards the light. And as Puckel sang, softly his stick slid down from the wall of the room where it had been propped and silently, slowly, glided across the floor towards the bed. It had become a snake.

Kittel did try to speak. She felt she ought to warn Puckel that the stick wasn't behaving as sticks should. But she couldn't speak: her tongue seemed to have stuck to the roof of her mouth, and not a sound would come out. Slowly the snake reached the bed and raised its head. Silently its neck stretched, waved to and

179

fro and stretched again, and silently its body followed, up the leg of the bed, on to the cover, and over the mound of Bull's feet.

Puckel never paused in his singing, and never looked towards the snake. The snake stretched its way up Bull's body, and when at last it lay on top of him, along his length, with its head at Bull's throat, it grew still.

All that long, dark night, as the snake lay stretched on Bull's body, Puckel sang, or was silent, or sang again. Dimly Kittel could hear people outside the room, shouting probably, or even banging at the door. But they seemed very faint and far away, and Puckel took no notice of them.

Through the window, behind the mountains, Kittel saw that the sky was growing paler. She had never stayed awake through a whole night, but this night she had not even felt like yawning, and now the dawn was growing and the day would soon be here.

Puckel's song had become quicker, full of a pulsing rhythm like a drum beat that made Kittel want to get up and dance. The snake was still motionless, but she could see that its lipless mouth was open and its tongue was flickering black over Bull's pale throat.

All of a sudden, Puckel jumped to his feet and abruptly stopped his song with a single clap of his hands. Bull's head was shaken out of his lap as he leaped up, but as it hit the pillow it moved twice, once to one side, once to the other. The snake's head reared up and drew back, as if it were about to strike at Bull's face. And suddenly Bull's still chest gave a great heave, and he started to breathe as if he were deeply asleep, while a soft, slight flush stole over his cheeks.

Kittel felt a thrill through her whole body. She had known all along that Puckel had great power, but until now she had not realized just how powerful he really was. When they had come into that room before, Bull's body had been dead. Now, it was certainly living. Kittel went cold and hot with amazement, but mixed with the amazement there was a little fear.

She had no more than a minute to think about what she had seen. Not then, anyway. For Puckel was still standing with his hands together over his head from clapping when the floor and walls and window all started trembling. It was a very quiet, slight trembling to begin with, but there was something about it which made Kittel think it was caused by something unimaginably strong. Puckel's triumphant expression changed. He froze, his hands still together, and glanced towards the window.

Kittel looked towards the window as well, where the dawn had filled all the air with soft grey light. The great round-topped mountain was humped black against the pale sky. But there was something wrong. Gradually Kittel realized that the whole land – with its forests and mountains – was shaking, as if something too big to even see had got hold of it like a table and was rattling it. And gradually, as she watched, the noise grew – a deep, drumming, thundering sound that became louder and louder until the whole house was vibrating and little puffs of dust plumed up round the edges of the carpet. Kittel clapped her hands over her ears to keep out the din.

And still the noise grew, until suddenly, with one gigantic *boom!* and a shock that hurled Kittel and Puckel back against the wall of the room, it stopped.

But out through the window Kittel could see an immense cloud of thick black smoke gathering and rising on a shoulder of the mountain, blotting out the sky. Fearfully, she grabbed Puckel's arm. "What is it?" she whispered.

Puckel made no answer. He gave a shout. Not a loud shout, though a very sudden one – and the window of the bedroom burst open. In fact, the whole window – glass, frame and all – simply blew out of the wall and smashed on the ground below. It seemed that Gogs' house wasn't having much luck with its windows: near by lay another scattering of glass where Cairo's head had broken the pane of Gogs' bedroom the night before.

Puckel and Kittel followed the window.

182

A Job for Kittel

Kittel couldn't tell how: one moment she was standing with her back to the bedroom wall – the next she was outside on the frosty grass beside the shattered window frame.

"Too late," Puckel was muttering, "just a little too late."

"Is it... Is it...?" Kittel whispered – she found she couldn't speak properly.

Puckel nodded his head. "The dragon," he said. "He's broken out."

Puckel looked at Kittel long and hard. He seemed to be saying something to her, without words, with his eyes. At last he did speak. "A job for you and a job for me," he observed. "Remember the first light of the sun! Now I must go." And with that he threw back his head and let out a shrill, piercing cry towards the sky.

"What about Sparrow? Where is he?" Kittel asked suddenly. At that moment a black, rushing shape came whizzing down from the air above. Kittel could not see it properly, though she could hear it – but whatever it was was coming straight for her head. She threw herself to the ground, and as she fell, she heard Puckel calling, "He was with the dragon!"

Nothing hit her. Nothing hit the ground beside her. She looked up, and saw no sign of Puckel. All she saw was a huge, wide-winged bird whirling off and upwards, in the direction of the smoke and the mountain.

Upstairs in the house, Kittel heard a sudden bang and then a shouting of excited voices coming through the empty window hole. Without stopping to think, she took to her heels and ran off towards Sparrow's house.

When she arrived back there, she felt weak and sick and trembling. She had to force herself to go on. First she ran round to the back of the house to check that Bull-in-Cairo's-shape was still there. He was – careering about the paddock in a frenzy. Whether it was the horse part of him terrified at an earthquake, or whether it was the Bull part of him realizing that the earthquake had been caused by the dragon, she didn't stop to ask. She looked at the sky. It was almost full daylight now, although she knew that it would be two hours still before the sun cleared the mountains and shone into the valley. She ran back round the house, and went in through the front door.

The house was empty. Kittel called for Murie, but there was no answer. It suddenly occurred to her that Murie was probably at her wits' end worrying where she and Sparrow had got to.

But there's no time to look for Murie, she thought, I've got to help Sparrow. She still didn't understand what had happened back at Gogs' house when Puckel had stared at her and told her she had a job to do. All she had known then was that she had to help Sparrow. Otherwise there seemed to be no clear thought in her head: she was like someone in a dream.

On the wall in front of her hung the crossbow which Sparrow's father had used. Like the telephone and the television and all the other things which lay unused about Sparrow's house, the crossbow was kept well dusted and polished. Well-oiled, too. On the wall beside it, the crossbow bolts looked fresh and deadly in their oiled paper wrapping inside the quiver. Unlike the telephone and the television, the crossbow still worked.

Kittel quietly went into the living room and fetched one of the chairs from the table. She put it against the wall of the hall and climbed on to it. She reached up and lifted the crossbow off its hooks on the wall. It was heavy but she could hold it easily enough in one hand. With the other hand she unhitched the quiver of bolts.

Kittel climbed down to the floor. She put the crossbow on the chair and gently eased out one of the bolts from the quiver. She ran her hand over it, and carefully touched its point. It was sharp as a newly ground knife, a heavy, deadly thing. Slowly, dreamily, as though she were asleep and someone else were moving her hands and arms, Kittel picked up the crossbow again and laid the bolt along it. Then she slowly wound back the string, painfully turning the

185

stiff mechanism until the bolt snapped into place with the string snugly behind it. The crossbow was loaded.

Cautiously, Kittel raised it and pointed it towards the wooden end-wall of the hallway. She looked along its length. Her finger was on the trigger, the bow against her shoulder. Her finger squeezed the trigger.

Zoomph! She staggered back, as the whole house seemed to shake with the force of the bolt. It had stuck fast, half buried in the timber. Without pausing, Kittel pulled out another bolt from the quiver, fitted it, and loaded it. Then she looked down at the quiver, wondering whether to take that too. No, she decided. One bolt was enough. Kittel left the house and went round to the paddock, carrying the loaded crossbow.

Cairo was no longer careering about. He was standing near the gate, almost as if waiting for Kittel. Kittel, numbed from lack of sleep, half in a dream, put her hand on the latch of the gate. "Time to go, Bull," she said.

"What's happening?" Bull asked through the horse's mouth, but he shuddered as he spoke. And Kittel understood then that the dragon did indeed have a firm hold on his mind.

"The dragon's broken loose," she answered.

"Time to go where?" Bull asked.

"Up to where the dragon is," Kittel replied.

"I may want to go there," said Bull, "but why do you?"

"I just do," said Kittel. "Will you take me?"

"Open the gate and you'll see," said Bull.

"Bull," Kittel said solemnly, "I know all about you and the dragon, and I just want to say this: I've been with P — the old man, I mean – all night, and I've just seen him bring your body back to life. It had *died*, you know, but it's all right now. P — the old man – sorted it, but it was all thanks to Sparrow. He's put himself into terrible danger so that you could get help. He may even be dead now. That's what your friend's like, Bull – that's what he'll do for you. Just like he let you have his magic gifts back at the start. He didn't have to let you have them, you know."

"I don't have them anyway," Bull muttered sulkily.

"Well, that's not his fault, is it?" said Kittel.

Bull was silent. It was impossible to know what he was thinking because he just looked horsy, but Kittel had a feeling that what she'd said had sunk in. Finally she asked, "Now are you going to let me ride on you up to where the dragon is?"

"I still don't know why you want to go," said Bull, after a pause.

"Nor do I exactly," said Kittel. "But I know I've got to get up there with you, as soon as possible."

187

Then Bull noticed the crossbow. "What's that for?" he said.

"I don't know that either," Kittel replied.

"You don't think you can shoot the dragon, do you?" he said, the horse's head trembling as he spoke. "Is it loaded?"

"Yes," she answered.

"Even I can't load one of them," – in his surprise, Bull's words came out like a whinny – "how could a girl load one?"

Kittel did not reply.

There was another pause. "All right," Bull said softly. "I'll take you."

Ten minutes later, Cairo was trotting smartly up the narrow forest track where Sparrow and Gogs and Bull had gone all those weeks before – on the day Sparrow had looked for Murie's stone and their lives had been changed.

Half an hour later, there could be no doubt about which way they had to go. The noise in the mountains was deafening. The trees were shaking this way and that, and great gusts of hot wind and ear-splitting roars came tumbling out of the air all around. But nearly another half-hour passed as they made their way through the forest, following the din, and they saw nothing until they came at last to the rise of land that overlooked the railway tunnel.

Nothing was happening at the tunnel mouth, but up in the forest in the other direction, Kittel and Bull soon saw what they were looking for. Indeed they could hardly miss it, for the air was full of smoke and flames, where a deadly fight seemed to be on between Puckel and the raging dragon.

The dragon must have been growing at a tremendous rate if it had still been in Puckel's bottle at dawn. Kittel wondered if it could get even bigger; as it was now, it was the most frightening thing she had ever seen.

Everything was in a flurry of confused activity, but after a while they could make out what was happening. Puckel was facing the dragon. Every other moment he was reaching out to either side, and immediately afterwards they would see a massive fir tree shoot up into the air where it would suddenly catch light and hiss and roar like an airborne bonfire, before crashing down beside the dragon, burning furiously.

Puckel was tearing the trees out of the ground! He was throwing them up into the air above the dragon, and every time he threw a tree, the dragon turned its head and set it alight. The burning trees were doing it no harm, but all the while Puckel was stepping slowly backwards and the dragon was advancing on him. Puckel was apparently distracting the dragon with the fir trees, and was slowly leading it towards the tunnel!

Kittel and Bull watched as, moment by moment, Puckel and the dragon came closer towards them. Kittel never moved, and neither did Bull. Quite possibly they would have waited there for ever, not knowing what to do, until the dragon had seen them and burned them up. But something happened which sent them into furious action.

Sparrow appeared. He came skimming over the forest towards Puckel and the dragon, but from behind the dragon, so that only Puckel could see him. He was carrying something.

At that moment, there was a change: a glint caught the corner of Kittel's eye. She glanced round, distracted from the fight. The top of the tall rowan tree down by the tunnel mouth was glowing with golden light. The first light of the sun was pouring through a gap in the mountains and lighting up the tree top. That's all very well, thought Kittel, but what place is not on the mountain and not in the valley? It was impossible – you had to be in one place or the other!

NOT ON THE MOUNTAIN AND NOT IN THE VALLEY

Sparrow awoke to the din of battle in the forest lower down the mountain. He lay for a minute wondering where his body was and how he seemed to be getting a vague picture in his head of Puckel and the dragon chasing each other through the trees, while crashings and roarings and tremblings of the ground went on all around. Then the reason came to him and he changed back into his own shape. The picture in his head, which must have been what could be seen from lower down the little dark stream, vanished, and he was standing in Puckel's courtyard of rocks.

I'd better find out what's going on, he thought wearily, and rose into the air. But he rose too high: he was blinded by the sun rising clear of the mist on the eastern horizon. He swooped towards the forest, which still lay in the shadow of morning, and very soon he spotted the cloud of dark smoke above the trees which must mark the spot where the dragon was.

He was not at all certain what he should do. He had no wish to get close to the dragon or the cloud of its poisonous breath, but on the other hand he felt rather guilty that he had let the creature escape. Should he fly down to the village and find out what had happened to Bull?

In the end he made for the scene of the battle. He selected a tree top that seemed to be reasonably free of smoke and flew down and settled in its topmost branches. He peered towards the forest floor, and began to make out what was happening.

What was happening was a most incredible game of hide-and-seek. Somehow, Sparrow knew that Puckel was there, and that he was shape-shifting, though there was in fact no sign of the old man himself. What there was instead were animals that appeared and disappeared, apparently leading the dragon on a crazy course down the tree-covered slopes of the mountain.

From his hiding-place, Sparrow saw a wolf spring out and snap its jaws at the dragon's toes; a mountain lion dropped down out of a tree and attacked the dragon's eyes. He saw another dragon break out of the ground and tear at the first dragon's throat. He saw other shapes and beasts he had never seen before nor could put a name to.

If this was Puckel shape-shifting, it was a kind of shape-shifting that was quite different from Sparrow's. Sparrow could only take the shape of things he saw already there. Puckel seemed to be inventing the shapes and then turning into them. Was this because Puckel was not inside the dragon's dream? Or was the dragon not dreaming at all, now that it was awake?

And soon Sparrow saw that Puckel was doing more than just turning into one thing at a time. The dragon was suddenly attacked by a fiery black bull on one side and at the very same moment by a giant lizard on the other. When it turned its head and snapped its teeth at the bull, the bull simply disappeared, and beside the giant lizard reared a giant brown bear, its red fangs snarling, while from the trees above swooped an osprey with raking talons.

None of the beasts harmed the dragon, as far as Sparrow could see, but they certainly kept it busy.

And then the whole forest suddenly seemed to be full of beasts of every shape, size, and description, and the noise of them all – snorting, grunting, baying, roaring, bellowing and bleating – rose even above the din of the dragon. Surely these beasts couldn't all be Puckel! It seemed impossible, yet Sparrow guessed that somehow, the old man had indeed transformed himself into all of them at once. And the dragon went quite mad, chasing this way and that on its huge, clumsy, scuttling legs, until it was out of sight amongst the trees. The rest of the animals romped off after it, hooting, howling and yammering.

In the brief quietness after they had gone, Sparrow flew down from his perch. Almost immediately he saw a large white billy goat trotting through the trees towards him. Its beard was so long it was brushing against its knees, and although it had very long, thick horns, it looked quite friendly. This was partly because its nose was so squashed-up and pink, which made it look very silly. The goat stopped and waggled its head from side to side. Sparrow could not help grinning at the creature. But then suddenly he remembered something, something from way back, something – in fact almost the first thing – Puckel had ever said. "Silly old goat." He could almost hear Puckel snapping it, apparently enraged at his own stupidity.

"You're Puckel, aren't you?" he said to the goat.

The goat went on waggling its head. And now there was something else. That silly old goat had...

"Puckel! You've forgotten your stick!" Sparrow cried. The goat waggled its head so hard that its beard whipped its knees. "Where is it? Oh!" – Sparrow ran his fingers through his hair in desperation – "It must be still at Gogs' house? In the room where Bull was lying? Is that it?"

194

The goat vanished. Sparrow blinked. Had he been dreaming? Did Puckel have his stick? What made him think he'd forgotten it? Why hadn't Puckel appeared to him in his own shape if he wanted to tell him so?

There was no answer to these questions, and Sparrow stopped no longer than a moment to think of one. If Puckel was busy with the dragon and didn't have his stick, Sparrow would have to fetch it.

Ten minutes later, Sparrow was at Gogs' house. He flew straight to the front door. He didn't care if anyone saw him.

But no one did. There was too much going on. Standing at the front door, Sparrow could hear that the house was in an uproar. Excited voices were coming from the kitchen, as everyone tried to shout everyone else down in explaining what was going on. He thought he caught Murie's voice amidst the hubbub.

He could also hear a noise outside, from lower down the valley. A large crowd of people were standing at the top of the road from the village. They were shouting as well, gawping and gazing up towards the great humped mountain where the black smoke had been seen after the earthquake at dawn.

Sparrow slipped softly into Gogs' house. He didn't bother to shape-shift: everyone was in the kitchen. Quickly and silently he ran up the stairs to the room where Bull had been. The door was open and he rushed on in...

And stopped dead. Bull was there all right, lying on the bed – Sparrow even noticed he was breathing. But sitting by the bedside –

Ms Minn! Sparrow could scarcely believe his eyes. There was his frail old teacher, with her trembly hands and her wild, wispy hair. Sitting on a chair beside the bed where Bull lay, she was looking Sparrow full in the face, but she said not a word. As Sparrow stood there, his eyes fixed on her in amazement, she nodded at him, slowly, silently as if she were saying, "Yes, that's how it is, and now you've guessed it, my dear..."

And as she nodded, Ms Minn faded. She became fainter. A second later, Sparrow could see through to the back of the chair she was sitting on. Another second, and she was gone altogether.

Puckel's stick stood propped against the chair. Sparrow was sure it had not been there a moment before. Could it be – Ms Minn – the stick? Was it possible? It flashed through his mind that the last two times he had found Puckel without his stick had been the last two occasions that Ms Minn had closed up the school... And then there was that last thing she had said – about having to go and see her brother... And then – the milkstones that he found each time she disappeared – one had even dropped from her coat... What was that crazy old woman? All that time, all those years when she had been going off alone and disappearing in the mountains, was that where she had been – in Puckel's cave, in Puckel's hand...? And what had been the movement near Bull's body when they had looked down from the cliff? The snake, surely – and was that why Ms Minn had not been at Puckel's cave that time?

Twice before Sparrow had been alone with the stick. On both occasions, it had behaved very dangerously. On both occasions it had seemed as though it were trying to kill him. Just for the very smallest moment the thought came to Sparrow that it might do something dangerous again; but almost in the same moment, he realized that things had now changed for ever between the stick and him. Ms Minn had been there, where the stick was now – dear, gentle, mild old Ms Minn: he *knew* something about the stick now, even though he didn't understand it. And knowing that something, he knew the stick would never harm him.

He wasted no more time on it. He grabbed it, leaped out of the hole where the window had been, and flew like the wind back towards the mountain.

When he found Puckel, Puckel had stopped changing into animals and was throwing trees about instead. They were quite near the railway tunnel, and not far off Sparrow saw Kittel sitting on Cairo's back.

"Throw it!" shouted Puckel, and Sparrow threw the stick to him. It whizzed over the dragon's head towards Puckel's outstretched hand. Light it was to throw, as any stick, but as it curved in a low arc over the dragon's head, Sparrow seemed to see in it a whole variety of different things: a stick, certainly, but also a coil of silver rain such as you see drifting through the mountain valleys on a grey autumn day; a brown and red snake with wings held close in to the long, sinewy body; and – yes, there was no doubt about it – an old woman with hair as wispy as mist... Surely that stick was the most mysterious thing he had come across yet!

But even as these stray thoughts flashed through Sparrow's mind, the dragon threw back its great head, rolled its fiery eyes, and – *snap!* – the stick, or Ms Minn, or whatever it was, disappeared into its jaws.

Aghast, Sparrow swerved forwards, though he did not know what he could do. He could see Puckel there, frozen like a statue: even old Puckel had been caught out! How could he ever control the dragon now, without his stick? He couldn't go on playing tricks with it forever.

Snap! The dragon's jaws clashed again. What was it after this time? With a shock, Sparrow realized it was after *him*! And as Puckel stood there, frozen, unmoving, the dragon spun round like a gigantic flicked whip, and Sparrow fled, up, into the air, as a fiery blast swirled around him and singed his hair. Looking back, he saw the dragon stretching out its bat-like wings, starting to row them backwards and forwards. In a moment it would have left the ground, thought Sparrow, and then... He wondered how long he could go on flying, how high, how fast, how far, before the dragon caught up with him and turned him to a flying cinder. Well, at least he might give Puckel time to think of something.

He glanced back again. The dragon's fore-quarters had left the ground. It was beginning its slow, lumbering flight up into the air, though its tail still dragged on the grass. Soon it would gather speed...

But Sparrow had reckoned without Kittel. So, apparently, had Puckel. Kittel took in everything at once. She saw the stick disappearing, she saw Puckel at a loss, she saw the dragon whirl round and begin to chase Sparrow. Urgently she leaned forwards to whisper in Cairo's ear. "Bull," she said, "I've got one bolt for my crossbow. I'm going to use it on the dragon."

Bull shook Cairo's mane.

"You'll never manage," he snorted scornfully. "I told you before."

"Bull," Kittel whispered fiercely, "if I don't use it on the dragon, I'm going to use it on you."

"Why?" the horse's mouth gasped.

199

"Because either you're going to help me, right now, and do what I say, or I'm going to think you're the dragon's friend: and if you're the dragon's friend, I'll kill you – I will! It's now or never, Bull. Either you're on the dragon's side, or you're on ours. If you're on our side you'll help me now."

The horse's ears twitched and were still. "One simple decision, Bull," Kittel said. "Remember all Sparrow's done for you. I know you think the dragon's wonderful, but are you going to watch it kill your friend? Do you think so much of yourself?"

Bull was still. It was impossible to be quite sure what he was thinking about the dragon. Horses' eyes always look a bit wistful, so it would be wrong to say that Bull was gazing wistfully at the great, terrible creature. It was impossible to know why he had agreed to come up into the mountains with Kittel: to help her, or to get nearer to the dragon. Kittel didn't want to think about it; she just waited. But Bull thought – for hours, it seemed (although it was really only a couple of seconds) – agonizing hours while the wind whipped round them in the winnowing of the dragon's awful wings. Slowly, inexorably, its legs, body, and massive tail were rising clear of the ground. Then –

"All right, let's get on with it –" Bull spoke through Cairo's mouth, and immediately trotted forwards.

Not on the Mountain...

Kittel sighed with relief. "One simple decision..." She knew now that, whatever was about to happen, Bull's mind would be safe from the devouring mind of the dragon. Cairo trotted on. *He's much braver as a horse than he would be as a boy,* she thought, and then she raised the crossbow.

"Faster!" she called to Bull.

Cairo cantered. Kittel squinted along the crossbow, but the horse's canter was making it too bumpy to aim.

"Faster!" she called. And Bull galloped. That was better! Kittel could hold the heavy crossbow steadier now.

Kittel never knew how she did what she did that day. She had never galloped bare-back on a horse before. She had never aimed and fired a crossbow before. But that day she did both at the same moment. She thought she must have borrowed some kind of magical power, that morning of the fight with the dragon.

The dragon had left the earth. Its flapping wings were creating a whirlwind on the ground below, and the trees were tossing wildly. It rose slowly, beating up after Sparrow, who was now distant in the air. It took a long time to get off the ground, but once it had got going Kittel knew only too well how fast it could fly. Sparrow didn't stand a chance.

Kittel, galloping towards the dragon, saw its grey belly lifted behind its massive chest. There

201

was a cleft running down the middle of its belly. That's the place, she thought – and fired. Her finger seemed to choose its own moment for pulling the trigger.

Straight for the dragon Kittel's one-and-only bolt flew. Straight for the cleft in its belly. And soundlessly into the dragon's belly it disappeared.

Kittel had believed Bull. She had never thought she could kill a dragon. And she was quite right. But what she did not know was that her crossbow bolt went straight through the thin hide on the creature's belly and clove into its liver, and that was like a long sharp icicle thrust into its tenderest part. The dragon let out an almighty roar, so loud that the trees split and an avalanche of rocks broke loose on the hillside. The arch of the railway tunnel collapsed and stones and earth filled up the tunnel mouth in seconds.

The dragon glanced down, searching out its unexpected attacker, and then swooped, coughing, gasping out great gouts of black smoke. Round and round like a helter-skelter it came down on Kittel, and suddenly Cairo's legs were knocked from under him as the end of the dragon's tail caught him like a lasso and sent horse and rider spinning off over the ground, past the glowing rowan tree, past the tunnel mouth, over the railway line, over a stretch of open grass to –

"Watch   out!"   screamed   the   horse. "We're –"

And Kittel did watch out – but there was nothing she could do about it. They were teetering on the edge of the cliff, with nothing below them but the empty air and little fir trees dotted about on the distant floor of rocks.

A split second they teetered, and then with a scream from Cairo and a scream from Kittel, they were over the edge, falling, falling, falling.

Kittel closed her eyes tight, hung on to Cairo's neck, hung on to the crossbow, and wondered if she would feel the crunch when they hit the ground. A bit of her felt annoyed that she was going to die when there were still so many things she wanted to do – telling her mum and dad that she was safe was the first of them. But another bit of her was not thinking that sort of thing at all. It was just falling, falling.

In fact the falling didn't feel too bad: it was like going very fast down a roller-coaster. In fact, falling off a cliff really felt quite pleasant, once you had time to get used to it...

Kittel opened her eyes. The ground wasn't rushing up to meet her. She was looking into the sky.

"I'm flying," she said aloud. "I must be dreaming. I must be dead."

"No, you're not," said Cairo's mouth. "You're alive."

"Sparrow?" said Kittel. "Is that Sparrow?"

"Yes, it's me," the horse's voice came. "I changed into Cairo when I saw you going over the edge."

"I didn't know you could fly when you were in Cairo's shape," said Kittel.

"Nor did I," said Sparrow. "I just knew that if you were going to be smashed to pieces, I wanted to be too."

"I feel funny, I'm going to faint," said Kittel.

"Please don't," said the horse's voice. "You'll fall off."

"All right," Kittel whispered. But she let the crossbow slip from her hand.

The horse flew higher. Kittel saw the dragon sprawled near the ruined tunnel mouth not far below. All in an instant, she noticed that its jaws were standing apart and Puckel had rushed forwards to grasp something in its mouth.

She felt more dreamlike than she had felt all that dreamlike morning. She understood exactly what was going on. Her arrow had not damaged the dragon, but it had made it cough and retch. And now it had coughed up Puckel's stick and the stick had got wedged between its jaws, and Puckel was going to pull the dragon by the wedged stick...

Higher they flew, and all of a sudden Kittel saw Cairo's dull brown back turn to glossy chestnut, while his mane turned to gold.

Of course, Kittel thought faintly: the first light of the sun – and in mid-air. Neither on the

mountain nor in the valley, it was so obvious!
And as she thought it, the horse under her gave
a shudder, then a great sigh, and flew on. To
Kittel, the change was obvious. A minute
before, Sparrow and a squashed-up Bull had
inhabited Cairo's body; now there was just
Sparrow.

And at that moment, in the upstairs room in
Gogs' house, Bull's blue eyes opened and he
looked about him. The sun reflecting off the
high mountains cast a rosy light on the walls
and the bedcover, although down in the valley
it had not yet risen. Bull stirred and sighed and
looked about: everything felt right. He tried
out his arms and his legs: they moved. Everything moved. But if Sparrow or Gogs had seen
him in that moment they would hardly have
recognized him: the closed doors of his eyes
had been broken open, and he looked as contented as a baby. The nightmare was fast
fading – the nightmare of animals that gib-
bered human words, of having a body that
couldn't keep its proper shape...

Kittel knew none of this. Gradually her
arms loosened round Cairo's neck and her
knees loosened where they had been gripping
Cairo's sides. "Here I go," she murmured, and
tumbled off the horse's back in a dead faint.

Sparrow became aware of her a second
later, falling down below him. There was only
one thing he could do. He could never fly

under her and catch her in Cairo's shape.
There in mid-air he left the horse's shape and
became himself again, swooping down to
Kittel before she fell too far away into the
abyss below.

He caught her long before she had reached
the tree tops and, holding her in his arms, he
flew up again. At the same time he heard the
scream of Cairo's voice, the one word "Master!" as the old beast went plummeting down
and smashed through the trees. The crossbow
and old Cairo had been the only things left
which had belonged to Sparrow's father, and
both were suddenly lost together; now the
paddock behind the house would always be
empty. Sparrow's eyes felt hot and pricking
and he found he was muttering, "I'm sorry, I'm
sorry," in answer to the horse's dying scream
that echoed over and over in his ears. "Master!
Master! Master!" Had he been given the gift
of understanding animals just to hear that?
"I'm sorry, sorry," he howled, as tears poured
from his eyes and splashed on to Kittel's head.

Sparrow hardly thought about where he
was going. The place where they landed at last
was none other than the courtyard outside
Puckel's cave, near where the little dark stream
came bubbling up out of the rocks. And Sparrow never even wondered that he had reached
it for the second time by flying. "I'm sorry," he
groaned, "I'm sorry."

Not on the Mountain...

Kittel, who had recovered from her faint, seemed to understand that Cairo was gone, and why. She stood silently with Sparrow beside the little dark stream and held his hand till his tears turned to sobs, his sobs to rough heaving breaths, and at last he was quiet.

It was from here that they saw the last of the fight with the dragon.

It appeared high in the air above them, locked in combat with old Puckel. Puckel was holding the dragon by the stick wedged in its teeth, as if the dragon were a fish on a hook. The dragon thrashed and roared, but though clouds of smoke kept belching from its nostrils, it seemed to have lost its fire. Below it, its long tail whirled round and round, coiling and coiling in a demented spiral. Higher and higher Puckel and the dragon whirled, and higher and higher again, until they were no more than a tiny coiling black spring up in the clear blue air. And still they went up, coiling and – very faintly now – roaring, until at last they could be seen and heard no more.

Bloop! came from Sparrow's and Kittel's feet. Then, *bloop!* again. Great bubbles of air were coming up from below the ground in the water of the little dark stream.

Bloop! The stream faltered. The water was becoming less. Minute by minute there was less, until only a trickle was pushing up through the flat stones.

207

Then, *bloop-schschschschsch...* the water stopped. The little dark stream had dried up.

Sparrow looked round the rocky courtyard. There was no sign of Puckel's cave, not a crack, not even a hollow. It was as if there had never been magic there.

"I think Puckel's gone away," he said in a slightly wavering voice.

"I know he has," Kittel answered.

"I don't think he or the dragon will be back," he said.

"I know they won't," said Kittel. "Let's go home now."

"You know what that means," Sparrow said – and now his voice was wavering in earnest – "it means that the dragon-mist will disappear, and your people will be able to come and look for you, and then you'll be taken away, and —"

"Hush," said Kittel, "we don't know what's going to happen." And Sparrow hushed, but he kept biting his lip.

After a while he said, "Maybe Cairo thought he was going back to his master. Maybe he's happy now."

"I'm sure he is," said Kittel.

Just before they turned to go, his eye caught something gleaming amongst the flat stones where the stream had once emerged into the light. He went down on his hands and knees and peered.

Suddenly he laughed. He put his hand between two stones and drew out a small piece of rock. Two fragments of glass tumbled off it and fell with a tiny tinkling sound in the dead quiet of the courtyard. "It's heavy!" he gasped.

Kittel looked at the piece of rock. It was like a little rough pyramid, and when you first looked at it, it seemed to be made of just ordinary stone. But as Kittel stared on, she realized there was something a little strange about it – almost as if, somewhere deep in its core, there were a glowing light. "What is it?" she said.

"It was a mountain," Sparrow grinned. "Puckel's been forgetful again: when he shrank the dragon, he shrank a bit of mountain too by mistake, and it went into the bottle. He said you shouldn't ever do that to bits of mountains, and he meant to put it back after he'd got rid of the dragon."

"He won't do that if he never comes back," said Kittel.

Sparrow chuckled. "Then I'd better keep it for him, hadn't I?"

As Sparrow flew with Kittel towards the village, they saw two small figures making their way through the open birch woods near the railway line – one dark haired, the other red. Sparrow turned towards them and came to land not far away. He rubbed his face which was itching from dried tears, and wondered anxiously how he should speak to his friends.

For the first time Sparrow could ever re-member, Bull hung back and appeared to be shy. It was Gogs who came forward and said, "Is this her?" looking at Kittel in some amaze-ment.

"I suppose so," Sparrow answered, remem-bering that Gogs himself wouldn't have seen Kittel but had probably heard about her from Bull. "She's Kittel," he added.

"Skittle?" said Gogs in even greater amaze-ment.

"I told you," Bull interrupted from behind him.

"Bull says it's six days since – since –" Gogs faltered.

"I know," said Sparrow, looking at his feet.

"I can't believe I've been asleep so long," said Gogs. "I've missed all the excitement."

"Can you still understand beasts and birds?" Sparrow asked uncertainly.

Gogs shook his head and grinned – the same old silly Gogs-grin they had always known. Nothing could change Gogs, Sparrow thought to himself. "Neither of us can," Gogs said. "Can you?"

Sparrow nodded. His third gift seemed to have slipped into his life almost without his noticing. Apart from the owl and Cairo's dying scream, he had not heard any birds or beasts talking – he hadn't had time. Now he became aware that there was a murmur all about him, like a hint of distant voices, that he only had to stop still and listen to: a whole unknown world waiting for him...

"I can't even remember what it was like," said Gogs.

Sparrow shook himself. "What?" he asked.

"Hearing the animals talk," Gogs said. "I can't remember it. It's like a dream."

"Oh," said Sparrow. "It's a bit odd, really..." He tailed off, listening again.

"I'm glad," said Gogs decisively. "I mean, we don't mind if you – I mean —"

"I want to say it," Bull broke in.

"Go on then," said Gogs, and turned red.

Sparrow found he had turned red as well.

"I want us to be friends again," said Bull.

"All right," said Sparrow, a little doubtfully.

"I know we can't be just as we were before," Bull went on. "But nearly – as nearly as we can manage..." Bull's expression was almost pleading.

Sparrow relaxed and smiled. "All right," he said again.

"It wasn't really Gogs," Bull said. "It was just me. You should stay friends with Gogs anyway. I should never have tried to get your gifts. They were yours. I'm sorry – I've been wrong all the time. I almost died. Twice, I think." He gulped. "Just being alive's better than having magic gifts – for me, I mean." He had been looking somewhere around Sparrow's stomach as he said this, but now he looked him full in the face, and Sparrow saw that his bright, piercing eyes no longer had their old command. They were a little bleak, perhaps wiser, certainly sadder, and – Sparrow realized with a shock – Bull looked up to him now. Sparrow had something that Bull knew he could never have. "I'm sorry and I'm glad too," Bull said firmly. "I mean – I think you deserve to have magic gifts. I don't."

And fixed with Bull's keen stare, Sparrow, as so often before, didn't know where to look – but now it was for a new reason.

"Perhaps if we ever see Puckel again –" he began, and then realized what he had said.

"There," said Bull. "That means we won't. Or at least, not to get magic gifts from him." Then he added, in a strangely solemn voice, "That part's finished."

"What do you mean?" said Sparrow. Did Bull still know something he didn't?

"I'm not sure," said Bull quietly. "Really, I don't know anything about it. But I feel – down inside – that something's just starting. I don't know what: something that's to do with all of us."

"That's what I think too," said Gogs. "And Skittle's arrived as well. That must mean something."

"It's Kittel," said Kittel tiredly. "Kay —"

212

"Well, I think it means something anyway," said Gogs.

"For one thing," said Sparrow, "I don't think Ms Minn will be coming back. We won't have a teacher any more. So I think instead we ought to get Kittel to teach us all the things she knows. And Bull as well – if you want to, that is."

Bull nodded slowly. "Yes, I'll do that. There're a lot of things I could tell you. But why do you think Ms Minn won't be coming back?"

And then Sparrow told them all he suspected about Ms Minn and the stick. And as the four of them returned to the railway line and set off homewards, stepping slowly, sleeper by sleeper, they talked over the whole adventure, gradually piecing things together. At the end of it, though, they found they still had no answer to the business of the milkstones.

"Maybe they were really snake's eggs," said Kittel, "and they hatched out."

"What into?" said Gogs.

"Baby Ms Minns?" Kittel giggled.

"They felt like stones to me," said Sparrow.

"Now Sparrow's the best stone-*loser* there is," said Gogs brightly.

"Sparrow's lost three stones," said Kittel, "and got three magic gifts. That doesn't sound like a bad swop to me."

"I wish Murie saw it that way," said Sparrow

ruefully. "And I'm going to have to explain about poor old Cairo and the crossbow too."

They went on down, until in an old orchard the railway line stopped and a wide track of grey-frosted grass continued in its place. Sparrow halted on the last sleeper and looked down to where the first houses of the village could be seen between the bare boughs of the apple trees. "There's one other thing," he said.

"What?" said Kittel.

"Well," said Sparrow, "When I first met Puckel he said I was in a dream. I know what he meant now. Because we were all in a dream, like Ms Minn said – the dream of the dragon. But what about now? The dragon woke, and I suppose it must be up there, up among the stars..." He stared into the wintry blue sky.

"And..." Kittel prompted.

"And that means," Sparrow went on, "that we can't be in its dream any more."

"That's right, because it woke up," said Gogs.

"So – I don't know what that means," Sparrow tailed off. "I don't really feel any different – not because of that, anyway."

"In magic," said Bull, "there are a lot of things you can't explain."

Sparrow shrugged. "I suppose so," he said. He stepped off the sleeper and continued on to the grassy track into the village.